Fate

The Perfect Time for Love series

Also by Natasha D. Frazier

<u>Devotionals</u>

The Life Your Spirit Craves

Not Without You

Not Without You Prayer Journal

The Life Your Spirit Craves for Mommies

Pursuit

<u>Fiction</u>

Love, Lies & Consequences

Through Thick & Thin: Love, Lies & Consequences Book 2

Shattered Vows: Love, Lies & Consequences Book 3

Out of the Shadows: Love, Lies & Consequences Book 4

Kairos: The Perfect Time for Love

<u>Non-Fiction</u>

How Long Are You Going to Wait?

Editor: Chandra Sparks Splond

Cover design by BJ Benjamin O'Neal (I Imagine Beyond)

For autographed copies, please visit:
www.natashafrazier.com

Acknowledgements

My biggest thank you is to Jesus, who orders my steps, forgives my sins, and blesses me with the time and ability to do the thing I love.

My husband, Eddie, and my children Eden, Ethan, and Emilyn – thank you for your love, support, and understanding (somewhat) of my writing time. 😊

BJ – Thank you for contributing your awesome design skills to create my covers.

Chandra – Thank you for your editing expertise.

Dearest reader – Thank you for supporting me by reading, writing a review, and sharing my books with others.

Chapter 1

The nightmares of Natalie Davis' death were slowly beginning to vanish. When Melanie Bennett finally pulled herself together, a song on the radio, a chick-flick about best friends, or a stranger with a strong resemblance would remind her of the last moments she spent with her best friend. A moment Natalie referred to as taking a break from the norm.

A moment that proved fatal.

Now, Natalie was gone forever.

Melanie had been a zombie at her hair salon, going through the motions of styling her clients' hair, not providing the spiritual advice they were used to receiving from her. She chimed in on conversations at the right time with the occasional *What, really, sorry*, and a few other simple phrases she relied on so her clients wouldn't feel ignored.

She merely existed.

But no longer was she the woman who had allowed unfortunate events to keep her from her greater self. After countless hours of therapy, she felt a bit better today. A vigor she hadn't experienced in a while. The holiday season tended to have that effect on her, no matter the circumstance, and today she was swept up in the joy and hope that often came along with the Christmas season.

Alone in the salon with nothing but R&B Christmas music and fragrant shampoo, conditioner, and hairspray to keep her company, Melanie sat in the styling chair dabbing her short natural ringlets with curl cream while she waited for her next client. Though drastic, she'd cut off her relaxed hair as a symbol of letting go of the past.

The door chimes signaled Charise's entrance. "Hey, Mel. Sorry I'm late. I brought you coffee." Charise, her long-time friend, rushed in and handed the caramel latte to Melanie.

Melanie eyed Charise's splitting ends and dry tresses. "Thanks!" Melanie smirked, graciously accepted the warm cup that satisfied the coffee lover in her and embraced her friend. "I'll give a little grace since you brought me this," she waved the cup in the air, "and drove from the other side of town."

"Yeah, I figured I could make up for my tardiness with the brew." Charise tossed her hat, purse, and jean jacket onto the armless loveseat, and plopped down into the stylist chair. "How are you feeling?"

"Pretty good. Thanks for asking." A sincere smile spread across Melanie's face — more sincere than she'd been able to muster in months.

"Your eyes are glowing. I'm glad you're in better spirits these days. You deserve some happiness."

"Thanks, Charise." Melanie's heart swelled and an even broader grin emphasized her cheekbones. Her inward transformation was apparent in her face, and the fact that someone noticed was progress. She rested a hand on Charise's shoulder briefly and Charise covered it with her own.

"You're welcome, honey."

Melanie tousled through Charise's shoulder length crumpled hair and pumped the salon chair with her foot. "What are we doing today?"

"The usual. Wash and curl." Charise mimicked scissors with her fingers. "I think it's time for a trim, too."

"Yeah, I'll take care of your split ends."

Melanie escorted her to the shampoo bowl and began to work her magic while Charise talked about everything that came to mind, including TV shows, her children, work, and politics. Melanie had long accepted that her clients considered her to be more than a hairstylist; she'd become confidant, counselor, and closest friend. Charise was known for not allowing much room for Melanie to get a word in. Being a stay-at-home mom, Melanie understood Charise needed time to chat about anything grown folks could understand, no matter what it was, so Melanie didn't mind the nonstop conversation.

Charise's chatter ceased at the sound of a tap on the door. Melanie called out to the person to enter, thinking it strange to knock. She and the stylists in the other salon suites were well enough acquainted to come in without waiting for an invitation. When the door creaked open, her stomach twisted into knots and the air trapped in her chest.

"Hi. We're hosting our annual…" Detective Brian Morris began but stopped and smiled like a game show contestant winner when he locked eyes with Melanie. "I didn't know you worked here." His head tilted slightly but his eyes remained glued to hers, and the warmth from the coffee she'd been sipping seemed to course its way through her body again.

"Yeah, this is my shop, Styles by Mel. I would shake your hand, but..." Melanie nodded toward the shampoo bowl and her hands, which were covered in shampoo and Charise's hair.

"No, problem." Brian leaned into the doorjamb, his eyes piercing her soul. "By the way, I love the new hairstyle." Brian jutted his chin toward her. "Beautiful."

"Thank you, Detective." Her voice pitchy and the corners of her lips pulled higher.

"The pleasure is indeed mine and please call me Brian." He cleared his throat. "If you don't mind, I'll leave the flyer on the table here. Hopefully, you can stop by Saturday."

"Stop by where?"

"My bad. I guess I was so surprised to see you I didn't finish my thirty-second pitch. We're having a toy drive in the Sevier Park community center parking lot, and we're asking local businesses for their support."

"Sounds good, Brian." Melanie emphasized *Brian.* "I'll check my calendar and stop by if I can." Melanie turned off the water to distract herself from his penetrating gaze. "Slow around the office these days?"

"Huh?" A fleeting frown flashed across his face.

"You're taking on the job of the mailman by hand delivering flyers instead of being Inspector Gadget."

Tickled at her joke, they both shared a hearty laugh, one Melanie needed. Charise, who normally had so much to say, was completely lost but managed to lift her head from the shampoo bowl to get a good look at the chocolate-six-foot-two-inch-athletic specimen that graced the entrance of the suite's doorway.

"And you're funny too." Brian's eyes narrowed and his eat-your-heart-out smile spread wider.

Was he ticking off a list of her qualities in his head?

"No, volunteering on my day off is all. I need to get going though. I've got a few more of these to hand out. Hope to see you at the toy drive this Saturday." He shot her one long, lingering look before he stepped out of her salon and closed the door behind him.

Charise lifted her head from the sink once more, slung water on Melanie, and exploded. "Mel, Mel, Mel! What was that all about? How do you know him? He is fine. Why haven't you scooped him up yet?"

"Woman, get back in this bowl, and mind your own business." Melanie attempted to blow her off.

"Must I remind you that while I'm in your shop, you are my business? Spill it. You know I live for love stories."

"First of all, there is no love story. He was the detective on Nat's case, that's all. This is the first I've seen him in about a year." Melanie's voice trailed off, and her thoughts went back to the day Brian and the other detective sat in her living room. He left the option open for them to stay in touch, but she didn't see any reason to. Besides, he only reminded her of losing her best friend. Those were memories she preferred to keep tucked away.

"Detective? Honey, the only thing he's trying to investigate is you!"

"You're so over-the-top." Melanie shook her head and shot Charise an I-can't-believe-you glare.

"I'm a woman with eyes! He is totally into you, and from what I can tell, you are into him too. I don't think I've ever seen all your teeth. Dude is in here for sixty seconds, and I saw your teeth, tongue, tonsils, and everything else you got in there."

Melanie chuckled at Charise's exaggeration. "C'mon back to the chair," Melanie instructed after she wrapped a towel around Charise's head. She wished she could change the subject, but Charise wouldn't let it go.

"Okay. How long have you known me?" Charise didn't wait for her to answer. "About twelve years, since we were freshmen at Tennessee State. You get quiet when you're uncomfortable, Mel, and try to avoid the topic at hand. But you had plenty to say a few moments ago when Mr. Show-off-my-bulging-biceps-to-the-woman-I wouldn't-mind-protecting-and-serving stood in the doorway."

Melanie rolled her eyes heavenward but couldn't help laughing. "You're unbelievable."

"All I'm saying is give dude a chance, especially if he's asking for it." Charise whipped her head around toward Melanie and jabbed her pointer finger in the air. "And trust me, sista, he's asking for it."

"And in twelve years, you still haven't learned how to listen. He didn't say that. He invited us to the toy drive. He didn't mention going out."

"No, he didn't, but he wanted to. He was probably imagining how your pretty petite frame would fit snugly in his arms!"

Melanie playfully tagged her shoulder. "No you didn't just say that!"

Charise ignored her and continued. "And as far as him inviting *us,* honey, I don't even think he realized I was in the room. His eyes were stuck on you like hair gel taming edges."

Melanie chuckled again but couldn't disagree because his chestnut orbs had her hypnotized, the salon lighting illuminated them and his clean-shaven head.

"Let me finish your hair so you can find something else to do."

"Uh huh, but you're going right?"

"I'll go to the toy drive if time permits and see what happens—if he's even there. How's that?"

"Honey, you and I know he'll be there waiting for you. If he wasn't planning to be there before, I'd bet my house that he plans to be there now. Charise jabbed a finger in the air to solidify her point. "And you're going to make time permit if I have to load those kids in the car and come pick you up myself."

"You are a mess."

"An honest mess."

Chapter 2

"We Wish You A Merry Christmas" blasted through the speakers set up outside of the Sevier Park community center. The annual tree lighting ceremony, the Christmas festival, and parade were all set to jumpstart the Christmas festivities. Nashville Metro Police Department's cruisers were positioned along the curb in front of the community center to accept toy donations.

Brian committed to volunteering for the annual stuff-the-cruiser toy drive, especially after seeing Melanie a few days ago. He could only hope she would show up and that he'd be around to see her. The environment would be more relaxed, and hopefully, she'd see him for more than the detective who worked the case of her deceased friend.

What did she think of him anyway?

Given the circumstances in which they first met, he couldn't fault Melanie if she hadn't entertained any romantic ideas about him. But the way she encouraged him with her I-wasn't-expecting-you-but-I'm-glad-you-showed-up-smile told him otherwise. If she dropped by today, he'd make his intentions known.

He busied himself most of the morning helping when needed—moving a table here or there, helping a vendor or two set up tents, carrying chairs from one place to another. Anything that would keep his mind occupied from wondering and hoping he'd see Melanie today. Occasionally, he'd see people come up to the cruiser where he accepted gifts, and his heart would beat triple time at the thought of it being Melanie.

Get a grip.

When he saw her at the salon a few days ago, the last thing he wanted to do was walk away again without getting permission to call her. A conversation about his interest in her in front of her client. Bad timing.

"Hey, Morris, come over when you finish up with that," Officer Rollins called to him while he set up a tent for a jewelry consultant.

"What's up, man?" Brian called to him when he was within earshot.

"Wanted to show you something." Rollins waved him over while leaning over the trunk of the cruiser.

Brian stopped in his tracks and turned his attention away from Officer Rollins when Melanie approached with a large bag in both hands. To anyone else, the large bags would have obstructed their view of her in a cropped ocean blue jacket and matching jeans, but Brian didn't miss the way her eyes sparkled, her hair shimmered, and her caramel skin radiated in the sun.

"Let me help you with that." Brian all but raced to her side and relieved her of the gifts she carried. "We appreciate your support. I'm glad you could make it," he said, breathless.

"No problem. It's the least I could do to help." In silence, she walked alongside him to the trunk where they started to fill a second cruiser.

This could be a now-or-never sort of thing, Brian thought. What were the odds of him running into her at the salon? Wasn't there a saying that good things came in threes? This was the third opportunity he'd had to ask her out. Only God knew if he would get the chance to see her again.

"So, are you planning to stick around for a while, or do you have other plans today?" Brian stuffed his hands in his pockets and casually leaned against the cruiser.

"I've actually never participated in any community events, so I'll try to stay long enough for the tree lighting." Melanie twirled the curls at the nape of her neck around her finger and shrugged. "We'll see."

"Oh, it's really nice. I think you'd like it." Brian nodded in the direction of the tents and gave Melanie a rundown of the day's events.

An awkward silence passed between the two once more and Melanie averted her eyes, locked them in the direction of the holiday market. Instinctively, they strolled away from the police cruisers through the market area.

"So, how've you been since the last time I saw you, before I gave you the flyer?"

"It's okay. You don't have to tiptoe around it. You can say Natalie's accident." Melanie took a deep breath and looked up at him. "I'm not that fragile. But to answer your question, I've been okay. Some days are harder than others, of course. The nightmares are starting to fade, and I'm getting used to my new normal."

"I'm not a counselor or anything like that, but I don't mind being a listening ear if you need someone to talk to on tough days."

"Thanks."

He paused midstride and turned to look at her. "I mean that. I know it's an overused sentiment people often say when folks are going through a tough time, but I'm being sincere. You can call me just to talk if you need to."

Melanie raised an eyebrow and smirked.

Brian chuckled. "Okay, that could probably feel a little strange to call the detective who worked your friend's case just to talk about your feelings, so how about we meet for breakfast or coffee some time—to talk about anything?"

"Are you asking me out?"

They shared a laugh and picked up their stride.

"Am I that terrible at it?"

Melanie tilted her head so that their eyes met and batted her lashes. "No, you're not terrible. I just wanted to be sure because I'd like that." A sweet melody to his ears.

"That's good to hear."

No longer in the detective only zone.

Brian stopped when they entered the market area. "I'll let you enjoy the day while I catch up with Officer Rollins over there." Brian jabbed a thumb in the direction of the police cruisers. "Will you stop by to see me before you leave?"

"I can do that."

∞

Brian disappeared from her side. Melanie worked her best to keep from thinking of the handsome detective by pausing at every craft tent to look at wreaths, handmade soaps, custom jewelry, and homemade caramel candies. She even stopped to chat with the owner of a puppy clothing boutique, and she'd never owned any kind of animal, let alone a dog.

As she moved from booth to booth, all she could hear were Charise's words echoing in her mind: *He is so into you.* Charise may have exaggerated and boosted her up a bit, but her curiosity encouraged her to stop by the event in hopes she'd see Brian. Her womanly intuition was smart enough to know he liked her, but maybe not to the level Charise insinuated. Whatever the case, he intrigued her, and she wanted to know him outside of his role as the detective who worked her friend's murder case.

The morning seemed to dance by in Melanie's mind. Though she stood most of the day for a living, her feet ached— a reminder she hadn't rested since Brian left her side. She visited the craft tents, sampled apple pie–flavored cookies, peppermint this and caramel almond that. She went backward from sweets to meats. A locally owned market gave samples of their flavored hams and turkeys, enticing the town to purchase their holiday goods from them instead of the large chain grocery markets.

"Melanie, right?" Detective Shane McDaniels questioned while she stuffed her mouth with maple-honey ham.

Her eyebrows shot up in recognition when she turned to face him. She nodded and swallowed quickly. "That's right. You're the detective who worked with Brian, right?"

"Yes. That's me, Shane McDaniels. You look well. How are you?"

"Good." Melanie quickly changed the subject so he wouldn't do what anyone else would have done—feel bad for her and tiptoe around her feelings. She held herself together as well as anyone who had lost one of their closest friends. "This is my first time checking out this event and it looks like I've been missing out. It's nice. Are you here helping out with the toy drive too?"

"Oh no. I'm off duty today. I'm here with my wife." He turned to introduce Chloe who had ventured off to the next booth, captivated by handmade jewelry. "Well, she's over there with the long, green dress. With pockets. Had to make sure to note there are pockets."

Melanie chuckled and spotted Chloe. "Okay. So, you've been well?"

"Yes. Newlywed actually, so things are good my way."

"Congratulations. I'm sure I'll bump into you again. Good to see you."

"Same here," Shane said and rejoined his wife.

Councilman Taylor's voice echoed over the loudspeaker turning everyone's attention to the tree-lighting ceremony. Melanie moved closer to the area, taking in the excitement of small children and their parents who juggled keeping an eye on them and recording the ceremony with their camera phones. Twice, she had nearly been knocked over by a couple of toddlers. Stepping out of the way the second time landed her in someone's arms.

"I'm sorry." She turned to apologize to the person she'd bumped into to avoid the toddler who ran wild without regard to anyone else in the crowd, his mom following close behind, apologizing.

"You're okay."

Her eyes widened in acknowledgement of his voice and her cheeks flushed from embarrassment. Had it been anyone else, she would have moved on after he accepted her apology, but it was *him*.

She ran her hands over her dress and cleared her throat. "So, how is the toy drive going?"

"Way better than expected. We've filled four cruisers already. Thanks again for your donation."

"No problem."

The crowd erupted in cheers and applause at the lighting of the tree. Following the ceremony, Melanie and Brian intuitively walked together as the crowd dispersed.

"I'm going to head home now. Thanks for inviting me out today." Melanie removed her keys from her crossbody purse. "This turned out to be nice." She held her breath and waited for him to officially ask her out on a date. Sure, he mentioned it earlier, but this was his chance to prove his sincerity and make plans

"So, how about dinner and a movie or that breakfast we talked about earlier?" Brian asked, stuffing his hands in his pockets.

"I'd like that. When do you have in mind?"

"How about I call you later, and we can discuss details then? Is your number still the same?"

"It is, yes." Her heart and belly were in sync, turning cartwheels. She reasoned she deserved this feeling. She couldn't recall the last time she'd been excited about a date.

"You'll hear from me tonight."

They'd finally made it to her car, and he opened the door for her. Handsome and chivalrous. His proximity raised tiny hairs on her arms and awakened feelings in her that had been dormant for longer than she cared to remember. After she said her good-byes and left the Sevier Park community center, her thoughts bounced back and forth from the time she met him up until a few days ago. A moment that she could only describe as fate.

Fate that, under terrible circumstances, introduced them.

Fate that reconnected them again in her salon.

Fate that drew her to him in a way she couldn't explain.

Chapter 3

Brian parked and walked down the aisle toward the Dillard's entrance outside The Mall at Green Hills. The Salvation Army's Santa Clause costumed volunteers jingled bells, sang their version of "This Christmas," and shuffled from side to side like they'd rehearsed all week long. His previous thought to get inside as quickly as possible dissipated, despite the temperature ranging in the upper forties. Their harmonizing stopped him in his tracks. Their smiles and jovial spirits were contagious and drew the same energy from strangers, including him.

Brian stood there for a while nodding to the tune and even found himself humming for a minute or so. The vibration of his phone reminded him he had a short amount of time to get in the mall, find a gift for his mother, and get home to rest before he could be called in to work. He glanced to read the text from his mom saying she didn't have any wish list for Christmas this year. *Thanks for making this easier, Mom.* He stuffed a twenty-dollar bill in the donation bin and continued his journey into what he referred to as one of his worst nightmares—shopping in the mall during the Christmas season.

He'd already given himself a time limit of thirty minutes. If he didn't find anything within that time, he would buy a gift card. He always thought gift cards were so impersonal, and he wanted to show he cared about the gift recipient by putting some thought into the gift. That had always been a challenging task when it came to his mother though. She rarely told him what she wanted. He'd often settle for buying her a Dooney & Burke designer purse or fancy perfume, but he'd feel better about his gift choices if she would tell him specifically what she wanted.

Growing up, she'd always ask for peace and quiet when he and his sister would ask her what she wanted for her birthday, Mother's Day, Christmas, or any other special occasion for that matter. Now that he was grown and out of her house, she could get that whenever she wanted. It wasn't like he had children to take over to her house, and neither did his sister. The more he thought about it, he wasn't sure if he knew what she liked at all. She wasn't open about discussing her feelings and what she genuinely wanted, so he usually felt like he'd come upon a dead end.

He browsed the fine jewelry, shoe, fragrance, handbag, and makeup departments, not certain of what to buy. He hoped something would jump out at him.

"Is there something I can help you with, sir?"

Brian shook his head and declined the invitation. That was the third sales associate who had offered to help him during his second tour through the shoe department. A total waste of time. He left the mall empty-handed.

The minute he made it to the car and strapped himself in his seatbelt, his cell phone vibrated again. He regretted coming to the mall when he should have been home resting. His work duties picked up more during the holiday season, and the incoming call proved that point.

"Morris," he answered with his standard greeting and started the car.

He input the address given by a fellow officer into the GPS, said a quick prayer after the call ended, and hit start on the system.

Brian navigated to the crime scene with his thoughts mostly reeling about Melanie. Even off duty, work usually consumed him, but now images of Melanie took up more space in his mind. The brightness of her smile could compete with the sun. Her almond-shaped eyes etched in his memory. Was she as excited about their first date as he was? Did she often think about him? Would she be spending Christmas alone? Would this be the first Christmas they spent with one another?

Brian shook his head to rid himself of the notions. It had to be silly to think about her so much, and they hadn't gone on a first date yet, right? Had he asked her out months ago, the ideas wouldn't seem ridiculous, but he wasn't going to let his mind go down that path. He had redeemed himself by asking her out, and she agreed, so this was a fresh start.

Their conversation last night had been refreshing. He spent half of the time laughing at her jokes. She overflowed with positive energy, nothing like the spirit of the woman he met last year who'd just lost one of her closest friends. At that time, he wanted to make it all better for her if he could, but now he wanted to be some of the reason why she smiled. They talked over an hour, discussing everything from the Christmas festivities at Sevier community center, work, favorite foods and restaurants, movies, church, and their favorite things about Christmas before she bid him good night. He smiled at the memory before switching his thoughts to work when he made it to his destination.

He slipped the cruiser into park, hopped out of the car, and immediately joined the crime scene, finding the first officer who had arrived to get caught up on the details.

"What do we have?" Brian inquired, slipping on a pair of gloves, and kneeling beside the body on the concrete. He nodded and scanned the area surrounding the young woman for clues. Crime of passion was his first guess. The rookie officer thought it could have been a burglary/homicide, but experience told Brian it was much more than that. She knew her attacker. The crime happened outside of her home in an exclusive neighborhood. Jewelry, credit cards, cash, and purse were all intact. Nothing appeared to be missing from her home. There were no signs of forced entry, and the half-eaten dinner on the table had a place setting for two.

An argument that turned sour.

Brian took statements from two of the neighbors who lived on either side of her. One didn't hear anything because he said he was asleep. He worked the night shift at a local bar and had the night off, the first in a few days. The other who made the call heard the screaming match and found the body.

Standard procedure, he handed them both his card to call if they could think of anything else and went through the house once more before he left the crime scene.

He worked these sorts of cases long enough to know the bartender knew more than he let on. He'd be making a follow-up visit and looking into his story to see if it checked out. Crime seemed to never cease, but he hoped to catch somewhat of a break this month. This was the first time in a while he looked forward to having time off for the holidays to spend with the special people in his life.

Call him crazy, but he was ready to see if his connection with Melanie could turn into something lasting. Work had always been his top priority, but seasons change, and this season could bring about something greater.

The season for opportunity.

The season for love.

Chapter 4

As much as Melanie enjoyed a great movie, she and Brian decided to save that outing for a later time and use their first date night as an opportunity to do something fun while getting to know each other. With a little protest from him, she encouraged him to sign up for a southern-inspired recreational cooking class. Melanie had heard so much about the Dabble studio from her clients and looked forward to trying it out for herself. Dabble offered food tours, cooking classes, and painting classes. Since they signed up for the cooking class this time around, she'd be more than happy to try out the painting class if all went well this evening.

Melanie dressed in a pair of stretch skinny jeans with a chocolate lightweight sweater that matched her riding boots. Though she looked comfortable and confident, her stomach twisted in knots the moment her doorbell rang. She masked her anxiety with an I-hope-he-can't-tell-that-I'm-nervous smile when she opened the door and Brian greeted her with a bouquet of white roses.

"Hey, Melanie. You look beautiful this evening."

"Thanks, Brian." Melanie just-act-natural smile widened, and she fingered a tight curl at the nape of neck.

Brian handed her the bouquet of roses. "These are for you."

"They're nice. Thank you. You can come in for a moment while I put these away."

Melanie didn't go crazy over receiving flowers. In fact, she could do without them. Thankfully, he brought them in a vase because she didn't own one. Flowers in her care seemed to die much sooner than they were supposed to, but she appreciated the gesture and thanked him again when she returned to the foyer.

"Ready to get cookin'?" Melanie asked when she returned with her purse and keys in tow.

Brian spread his arms at his side, palms up. "About as ready as I'll ever be."

With each passing moment, her nerves subsided, and she became more comfortable. It helped they'd spoken on the phone the past few days instead of only sending text messages. They talked about their workweek briefly on the ride to the studio, though Melanie did the bulk of sharing— new clients who tended to pop up around the holiday season, a white elephant exchange between the stylists.

Brian didn't go into much detail about his work. Crimes happen every day was the way he put it. He shifted uncomfortably in his seat when she probed a little for more detail like talking about crime would set her off. It wasn't that she wanted details about the crime, more so of how he dealt with it personally, but she didn't press the issue.

When Brian and Melanie arrived at the quaint brick studio, they were immediately greeted by an associate inside, given matching aprons, and shown to their seats at a wooden table, some of which sat four guests. They were escorted to a table for two with ingredients already in place.

Brian helped Melanie into her apron and secured the string at the back, and she returned the favor. He pulled out her barstool and waited until she sat comfortably before taking the seat next to her. A cloth as white as a sheep's wool covered the table adorned with a bowl of flowers and two empty glasses. There were three white bowls, each filled with ingredients they would use to make tonight's dinner. One bowl contained seasonings and another shrimp. He couldn't identify the vegetables in the third bowl, which prompted him to pick up the menu.

"Have you made shrimp jambalaya before?"

"Once, but I'm almost sure I didn't use most of the stuff set before us." Melanie gestured toward the table with a wave of her hand. "But hopefully I can beef up my culinary skill, plus I'm hungry, so I'm hoping this is good."

"Same here." Brian shifted on the barstool until he faced Melanie and rested his clasped hands in his lap. "I've never cooked anything remotely close to this. My skills are limited to grilling, using the rice cooker, whatever vegetables I can buy in one of those steamable bags, and baked chicken or fish."

"Doesn't sound limited at all to me." Melanie turned to face him and crossed her legs, careful to maintain her balance on the stool.

"I mean, I'm not terrible. My mom made sure I wouldn't starve while living on my own or spend my days eating fast food."

"I'd like to try some of your cooking." Melanie clamped her lips shut and hesitantly flashed an I-can't-believe-I-just-said-that smile.

"Sounds like you're asking me out on a date. Is that what I'm hearing?" Brian teased, sensing her embarrassment when she bit down on her bottom lip a moment too late.

Melanie laughed and shrugged. "Let's just see how tonight goes. If you burn this place down, I may not want to be seen with you again."

It was his turn to join her in laughter. His easygoing spirit relaxed her. Until the instructor and every participant joined the class, they spent the next few minutes talking about their favorite foods again. Melanie shared grilled shrimp, any grilled fish, sweet potato fries, stuffed bell peppers, boudin, and chocolate cake topped her list.

"Welcome, everyone, I'm Chef Antonio Marques. Who's ready to have fun with food?" he asked, interrupting the light chatter in the room.

Brian and Melanie turned their attention toward Chef Antonio and waited for instructions.

"Here we go," Melanie said with a wide grin and wink.

Chef Antonio spent the next few minutes making sure each table had all their ingredients before he instructed them on what they should do first.

"As you all know, this is BYOB—bring your own bottle. You can start drinking at any time; however, I don't suggest you add whatever you're drinking to the recipe tonight. If you do, I am no longer responsible for the flavor."

Light chuckles erupted from the crowd as he continued.

"Everyone has a bowl of shrimp. Take two pinches of seasoning, sprinkle the shrimp, and toss lightly until covered. Take the seasoning packet and add its contents into the empty bowl. Bring your bowls to the stove in the back, and I'll give you further instructions on how to make the sauce."

Melanie and Brian followed the chef's instructions, worked quietly alongside each other, and shared a smile here and there. After they seasoned their shrimp, they emptied the seasoning packet and followed the chef to the back of the room along with twelve other guests.

"This is actually nicer than I thought it would be. I'm impressed," Brian leaned and whispered into Melanie's ear, a move that sent a tingle down her spine.

"Think you'd like to come back for painting classes one day?" Melanie asked.

"With you, yes." Brian's I'm-having-a-good-time smile matched hers.

Chef Antonio stood at the stove and demonstrated how to prepare the sauce, stepped aside, and motioned four guests to the stoves to prepare theirs. The room was equipped with two stoves in the back of the room, allowing two people to work at once per oven. When Brian and Melanie began, the chef complimented them both on their sauce's texture. Creamy.

"See, you're a better chef than you thought you were," Melanie said to Brian when they returned to their seats.

"According to Chef Antonio, I am. I just might have to take you up on your offer to have me cook for you."

"My offer?" Melanie threw her head back and chuckled.

Brian smirked and placed an index finger on his lips. "*Shhh.* I need to pay attention so I can step my cooking game up for you."

Melanie stifled a laugh as Chef Antonio took his place in the front of the room and continued with his instructions.

Brian took the rest of the evening seriously when he prepared his courses: shrimp jambalaya, side salad with Chef Antonio's homemade vinaigrette dressing, and peach hand pies.

"I have an idea. How about we switch? You can have my dinner, and I'll eat yours," Melanie suggested.

"But," Brian said wistfully, "we made the same thing."

"True, but you were working really hard, and this gives me," Melanie pressed her hand to her chest, "an opportunity to try your food before committing to have you cook for me later." Melanie wriggled her eyebrows.

Brian swapped their plates. "You know this doesn't really count. I had a lot of help."

"Yeah, but it's no different than you following a recipe at home in your kitchen." Melanie put a spoonful of shrimp jambalaya in her mouth. "*Ummm.* Tasty."

Brian also tried it and mimicked her reaction. "This is really good. Honestly, I'm enjoying this more than I thought I would. I'm glad we did this."

"Good. I've heard so much about it over the past few months from my clients. This has been a wonderful experience, and it helps that I have great company." Melanie took another bite.

"I feel pressured to come up with something to top this for our next date."

Melanie paused, the spoon halfway to her lips. "Next?"

"Am I getting ahead of myself?" His smile faded, his eyes widened, and his eyebrows lifted so high she thought they'd reach his hairline. His face relaxed when she smiled.

"Teasing. I'd love to go out with you again. I've enjoyed your company," Melanie reassured him with a quick pat on his shoulder.

"Same here." Brian's eyes narrowed and rested on hers and her stomach and heart seemed to have high-fived each other. Melanie took a sip of water to calm her nerves and break the trance he'd put her in.

Pull yourself together.

When their evening ended and Brian saw her safely inside her home, Melanie stood in the foyer, rested her back against the door, and listened to his footsteps trail off until they were non-existent. She smiled at the thought of him being the rainbow after the storm of Natalie. She hadn't been out on a nice date in two years, and it felt good to admire and be admired. She finally had great news to share with her therapist—she'd started enjoying life again.

Chapter 5

The Nashville Christmas lights tour had been on Melanie's list of things to do for years. Brian had the weekend off, and she adjusted her work schedule to experience the tour and enjoy more time alone with him this weekend.

Time that she looked forward to more than anything.

As a cosmetologist, Melanie had the luxury to set her own schedule. Thankfully, her clients had been flexible when she asked to move their appointments up which granted her the opportunity to leave much earlier than normal on a Saturday. She finished up with her last client, took a few moments to primp in the mirror, and closed the shop so she could meet Brian for the tour.

She cruised along Music Valley Drive humming to an India Arie playlist, passing several hotels until she could find a place to park that wasn't too far from the tour bus pick-up area. She spotted Brian in a cranberry cable knit sweater and blue jeans headed in her direction, checked her reflection in the mirror one last time, and applied a thin layer of lip gloss before she got out to meet him.

"Hey! Doin' okay today?" He handed her a Styrofoam cup of hot chocolate. "I thought you might like one of these."

"You read my mind. Thank you."

A cup of hot chocolate was perfect for the occasion. The warmth from the liquid coursing through her body matched the warmth in her smile. "I'm good today. How are you?"

"Even better now." Brian unfolded a plastic bag he'd been carrying, pulled out two striped candy cane Santa hats, and handed one to her. "Got this for you."

"Seriously?" Melanie's tossed her head back and chuckled.

"Yep. Got one for me too. See?" He slid his hat over his cleanly shaven head. "I know you're not going to have us out here all mix-matched. You have to wear yours too."

A little goofy, but still heart-stopping handsome.

"Well, in that case…" She carefully pulled the hat over her curls, curls she had spent thirty minutes perfecting earlier that morning. "Thanks."

"You're welcome."

Brian guided her in the direction of where the bus would depart, his hand gently rested on her back while they maneuvered through a crowded sidewalk. He bent down and whispered, "Don't worry, you're still beautiful." Her heart flipped like pancakes and she wore one of those he's-making-my-heart-melt kind of smiles, but he didn't notice because he stood at least a foot taller than her and his focus had been to get them through the crowd, or so she'd hoped.

The warmth from the sun kissed her cheeks, but the sudden change in wind speed made her regret she left her jacket. It was unseasonably warm for December, which led her to think she wouldn't need it, but the closer they got to the motor coach, the cooler it became. She was more than thankful for the cup of hot chocolate, which now served its purpose of warming her body as opposed to employing the holiday spirit.

Another force of wind nearly blew her hat off while they waited to board the bus, bringing with it the smell of grilled food. Her stomach growled, reminding her she'd worked through lunch to meet Brian for their afternoon date.

Brian looked down at her flushed face. "Hungry? We can skip this and do it another time if you'd prefer to get something to eat."

"I skipped lunch today, but I can wait a while longer. I've been looking forward to this tour for quite some time. Plus, this is my favorite time of the year, and I'd rather not put off any holiday festivities if I can help it."

Brian shrugged and smiled. "I've been looking forward to the tour as well but thought I would ask. Your stomach might disagree with you."

"Maybe, but I can keep it in check." Melanie patted her belly like the gesture would control the growling.

The two-toned red-and-black motor coach was decorated with garland and multicolored lights. The driver wore red and green with a candy cane–decorated Santa hat. Boarding the motor coach, Brian held out his hand to help Melanie up the steps. She stumbled a bit at the unexpected tingling sensation sending alarming signals to every inch of her being, gripping his hand tighter for a millisecond to brace herself. Her eyes trailed from their joined hands to his eyes. Recognition flashed within them.

Did he feel it too?

That sizzling spark of electricity.

He had to. Or was she imagining it? His *It-wasn't-just-you-this-thing-between-us-is-real* smile reassured the fleeting thought. Every feeling she experienced in the last few seconds was real, raw, and replicated.

Melanie found the nearest empty seat and quickly sat to hide her now trembling hand. Brian followed close behind, took the seat next to her, waited for the bus to fill and the tour guide to begin his announcements. His lips parted and closed, like he wanted to say something, but Melanie was glad he didn't because her mind was in overdrive.

What just happened between them?

Unexplainable.

Unfamiliar.

Undeniable.

Dressed in a red Santa hat with a bell attached and a green elf costume, the tour guide sang, "Merry Christmas" to which everyone returned the greeting before she gave a quick rundown of the tour route.

"We're not the only ones feeling festive." Brian whispered, leaned closer to Melanie, and nodded toward the tour guide. His lips close enough to her ear to send another current along the left side of her body with each spoken word. She shuddered and forced herself to focus on the tour guide.

Was she being weird?

Did he notice?

The two-and-a-half-hour tour took them through Franklin, Tennessee, the location of the Battle of Franklin during the 1864 Civil War. They had the opportunity to see the Lotz house, which stocked Civil War antique items. The decorations of the two-story, four-column Greek revival white frame building during the season was representative of Christmas during the Civil War era. Melanie had no idea the tradition was in place until the tour guide mentioned it when they rode through the area. The bus stopped to allow the passengers to get off and take pictures. Some passengers stayed aboard and snapped pictures from their seats, while Melanie and Brian, among others posed in front of the Lotz house.

The tour took them through some of the wealthiest neighborhoods in the area, many of which Melanie had no idea existed. Some of the over-the-top displays instantly reminded her of the television show that hosted the Christmas lights competition. The two-story house sat on an acre of land, and it seemed every inch was covered in lights—the house, the grass, the landscape, trees, light posts. If it was there, it was covered and beautifully done. *Merry Christmas* was written across the front yard in lighted letters about five feet tall. She'd snapped more pictures on her cell phone in two hours than she had in the last six months.

Along the tour they stopped for carolers and joined in with them for two songs. Every display along the tour was more festive than the last, from popular Christmas tales like Frosty the Snowman, Rudolph the Red-Nosed Reindeer, and the Elves and the Shoemaker to Christian themes like Joy to the World, Jesus is the reason, and the nativity scene which brought Melanie to tears.

"You okay?" Brian noticed her wet cheeks.

"Yeah, yeah, I'm good," she answered, her throat a little scratchy. "You'd think these are just lights, but they're so beautiful, and they remind me of God's beauty and admiration of me. Even if it were just me, God would have sent Jesus to earth by way of the Virgin Mary so He could reconcile me back to our Heavenly Father. This scene is such a sweet reminder of God's love."

A reminder that Melanie needed because of the losses she'd experienced in her life over the past few years.

"Indeed, it is. I'm glad I waited so long to do this because I get to experience it with you. Thank you for coming with me."

"I'm happy to be here with you, too." *There is no place else I'd rather be right now,* she thought, but wouldn't dare say it. She snapped another photo, then rested back against her seat, admiring the lights throughout the remainder of the tour.

Though they didn't get a chance to engage in much conversation, their hearts were satisfied as they began to experience the beauty of the Christmas season together.

Chapter 6

Melanie lay on the comfort of Dr. Williams' cream leather sofa, her head against the armrest. She'd never felt relaxed enough to lay down before today, but she was different. Besides, she usually had the feeling Dr. Williams looked through her and asked probing questions she didn't want to answer, though they needed to be addressed, hence the reason she decided to see a therapist. Natalie's death had taken a toll on her, and Dr. Williams helped her cope with her feelings.

The walls were painted yellow with a blue accent wall, a combination of colors Melanie wouldn't have put together, but they worked in Dr. Williams' office and somehow attributed to her feeling more comfortable when she walked in the room. That and the lavender scent. A vase of fresh flowers sat on the table next to the couch. A four-tiered bookshelf filled with different counseling theories and coping mechanisms of issues she'd never even dreamed of was in Melanie's line of view as she lay on the couch. She closed her eyes to focus on Dr. Williams' questions.

"You seem relaxed today. Do you feel relaxed?" Dr. Williams settled into her honey brown leather chair across from the couch.

"I am. Life has been treating me well for a change." She thought of Brian and instinctively, a smile danced across her face, but oh how she wished she could take back the end of her statement. Dr. Williams took everything she said seriously and would want to explore her feelings.

"For a change? Why do you say that?"

Doesn't she have a pad filled with notes from our sessions over the past six months? Melanie's eyebrows crinkled together, and she turned her head to see Dr. Williams resting her chin on her fist, her eyes boring into her soul. Yeah, she wanted her to respond to that question. But didn't she already know the answer? Melanie took a slow relaxing breath and closed her eyes again. "I met a guy. Well, we didn't just meet—more like reacquainted. He was the detective who handled my friend's case."

Dr. Williams waited for a moment to see if Melanie would say more. The periods of silence where the only sound she heard was Dr. William's scribbles on the notepad sometimes intimidated Melanie. Did she provide enough information?

"Tell me about him." Dr. Williams' voice was soft and comforting, encouraging Melanie to continue.

"He's kind and attentive. I like how I feel when I'm around him. The way he looks at me makes me feel like I'm the only person in the room. He seems gentle and cautious, which makes me think he considers his words carefully around me. Because of how we met, I think he avoids certain conversations or treads lightly, like I'm going to break at any moment. I asked him about his friends and what they usually do when they hang out. He responded, but didn't ask me about my friends, though he reciprocated other questions. He's a Christian, one who goes to church, serves in ministry, and works to live according to the Bible. That's important to me, and it's quite different. I haven't met many guys who are Christians who are fully committed to their faith. He also has a career he loves. He's a problem solver, so I think being a detective suits him perfectly."

Was she rambling? She paused for a moment and glanced at Dr. Williams who jotted more notes onto her pad and encouraged her to continue with a slight nod.

"He's gorgeous." Melanie's voice squeaked. She shared that like she was dishing to one of her girlfriends about her high school crush. "He has one dimple in his right cheek and a set of dreamy brown eyes. A cleanly shaven bald head." Was it as smooth as it looked? Melanie stopped to give Dr. Williams a moment to ask the probing questions she always had lined up.

"You mentioned he treats you like you're going to break at any moment. Let's explore that. Do you feel like you might break at any moment?"

Didn't she choose her words carefully? Dr. Williams had a way of honing in on words Melanie deemed insignificant. Melanie didn't move to look at her. She continued to lie on the couch with her eyes closed. The fresh lavender wafting through the room contributed to her calmness.

"No, no, I don't think that." She shook her head. "I'm just fine."

"What does fine mean to you?"

"That I can say Natalie's name without tears welling in my eyes. I can enjoy being in Brian's company without thinking about the circumstances surrounding how we met, and I no longer blame myself for Natalie's death, and I owe that to you." This time she opened her eyes and turned her head slightly toward Dr. Williams and smiled. "I want to thank you. I don't know how I would have made it through these last few months without you."

"Melanie, you've done all the hard work yourself." Dr. Williams closed her notepad, laced her fingers together, and placed them in her lap. Perfect posture. "It has been my pleasure working with you and it does my heart good to see that smile of yours, a genuine smile. Looking into your eyes, I can see that the weight has been lifted. You should be proud and because of your progress, I think it's time we change the frequency of your visits.

"Thank you, Dr. Williams."

Dr. Williams suggested they change her appointment schedule from every two weeks to once per month. Melanie had begun to cope with Natalie's death and move on with her life, which was the goal they'd set when she first began her sessions. Being amid the holiday season and Dr. Williams planning to take time off for the Christmas and New Year's holidays, Melanie wouldn't see her again until January.

Dr. Williams scheduled Melanie's next appointment, wished her a Merry Christmas and prosperous New Year, then escorted Melanie down the corridor to the exit.

Melanie arrived at the elevator bank, head down, engrossed in her cell phone, checking text messages and e-mails. Many of her clients wanted to rearrange their normal appointment schedules to see her before Christmas because they were traveling. She prided herself on not double booking or having more than two clients in her salon at once. The elevator buzzed and alerted her to its arrival. She lifted her head long enough to step onto the elevator and press the button for the ground floor. As the elevator doors closed, she caught a whiff of cologne that reminded her of Brian, which she attributed to her imagination since he was on her mind and she had recently finished a conversation about him with Dr. Williams.

Chapter 7

"Hey, Mom. Ready for lunch?" Brian asked. Purse on her shoulder with her key in the keyhole, his mother turned her cheek to accept a kiss from her son.

"Yes. I'm done for the day. How long do I have you before you're called away?"

"We should be good. Where do you want to go?" Brian hung an arm around her shoulder, which she managed to shrug out of.

Displays of affection somehow made her uncomfortable. He couldn't remember how or why she became that way. When he was a small child, even through most of elementary school, he could recall her pulling him into her arms for long hugs and kisses on his forehead. But like most pre-teens, he tended to run in the opposite direction when she wanted to physically display any affection. For him, words would do. When he became an adult, he didn't mind a hug and kiss to the cheek from his mother, but that was something he seldomly received. Though she accepted his affection, Brian didn't receive the same in return. He'd grown to accept that as her way, but it bothered him, and he didn't know how to express that without feeling weak.

"I'm free today. Want to try that new seafood place down the road? I've heard good things about it."

"That sounds good. Apparently, their lobster bisque is tasty. I'd like to try that. If it's good, I'll take some home for your father. He's working late for the next few weeks so he can relax a bit during the Christmas holiday. He mentioned something about getting the numbers to the accounting firm for the end of their fiscal year. All that accounting stuff is foreign to me. I'm past trying to understand that lingo. If I can have both of my guys home without interruption during this Christmas season, that's fine with me. Sharice won't be home this year. She's spending Christmas with her new boyfriend and his parents in Colorado." She turned to Brian and smiled weakly as he opened her car door for her.

"Should work out fine. Sharice will be alright. We can video chat with her on Christmas Day."

"I guess I don't have a choice, do I?"

Brian waited until he shifted the car into gear and pulled out into traffic to bring up Melanie. "Mom, do you mind if I bring someone over for dinner this year?"

"Mind? *Tuh!* It's about time. It's about time you started seeing someone. I think you could use some love and goodness in your life. If you keep working like you do and seeing all the bad there is in this world, it'll drive you mad."

"I think you raised me to have a pretty solid foundation in my faith. I'll be fine."

"I'm just saying, God didn't leave Adam alone—even he received a helpmate." She pressed a finger into his shoulder. "It's not such a bad idea for you to have one either."

Images of Melanie flashed through his mind, and Brian couldn't agree more. He turned slightly and a you-have-no-idea kind of smile spread across his face, but he didn't comment. His mom had a way of reading people, especially him, except when it came to his need for her affection. She was on point in her assessment of his desire for a wife. He could only hope this thing with Melanie would turn into something beautiful and lasting.

Brian navigated the car into the parking lot of Seafood & Things and quickly snatched up the parking space of a customer who left. He cut the engine and moved around to the passenger side to open the door for his mom, extending a hand to help her out of the car.

"How are things in the office?" He led her across the parking lot paved with rocks. "Be careful. Don't want your heels getting caught."

"Thanks." More focused on the rocks under her feet, she answered, "Office work is good, and clients are steady. Thanks for asking. Tell your detective friends I'm here for them if they need help coping with the ugliness they experience day-to-day. You know my slogan."

"Let the feelings out so the healing can come about," Brian recited along with her. "It's a bit corny."

"But it's true, and it works. Holding things inside doesn't help us. We must learn to express ourselves in the right way and seek our healing. So many of us rely on God for our healing but won't use the avenues He has created and allowed to help."

"I hear you. Table for two, please," Brian said to the hostess when they arrived inside, the aroma of seafood spices deepened his thoughts of Melanie and he smiled instinctively.

What reminded her of him?

"So, tell me about her. How did you two meet?" Pamela asked after they were seated and had given their drink orders.

"Work. I met her while I was investigating a case." He skipped the details because he didn't want to revisit that case nor did he want his mom picking apart Melanie before he introduced them. No doubt she'd work up ways to help heal her before she'd even met her. Not the topic of conversation he wanted at the Christmas dinner table.

Her raised eyebrows beckoned him to continue. "We didn't start dating around that time. I ran into her about a month ago and asked her out. She's a believer, so we have the same values. She's beautiful, giving, and tenderhearted. We get along very well. I'd like to see where this goes."

Does she feel the same way?

"It's been a while since you've dated anyone, so I think this is good for you. It's about time you've gotten past the hurt Penelope caused you."

"Let's not go there, Mom."

"We don't have to *go there,* as you put it, but you know my thoughts about healing from the past. If you care about this new woman, the issues you had with Penelope need to be addressed."

So much for not going there.

"I'm good, Mom."

"Not if you're still married to your career you're not."

Brian folded his arms across his chest and flexed his jaw muscles. Why were they talking about Penelope? She made her decision, and he did what he thought was best at the time. He loved her, but his career was important to him and she knew that.

"It wasn't like she didn't know what she signed up for when our relationship got serious. I have a demanding career, what did she expect me to do?"

"Love her, Brian. That is what all women desire."

"I did love her. That wasn't the problem."

Brian took a long gulp of water and thought back to the day she left. Penelope had broken off a one-and-a-half-year relationship. Though he believed they were well-matched, she had a laundry list of reasons why they couldn't work, and they all centered around his career — his career had more of his heart than she did.

Brian hadn't heard from her or seen her since. As far as he knew, she didn't even live in Nashville anymore. She'd changed her phone number and address. He didn't want the same thing to happen with Melanie, but he could already sense that wouldn't be an issue for the two of them.

"Not with one foot in and the other foot out the door. You have to be all in."

Brian took another long draw from his water glass. "I hear ya."

"I'll say this, and I'll leave it alone. As long as you dated Penelope, you never took time off work to spend a holiday with her. Your heart has been chained up, and I can't wait to meet the woman who has the magic key."

Brian chuckled. "Not magic. I can't quite put my finger on what it is, but I'm drawn to her, and there's no other explanation except God may be leading me to her."

Pamela smiled and reached across the table to cover his hand with hers. "I'm sure she's nice. The joy in your eyes and voice tells me so. Just don't forget what I said about going all in."

"Thanks, Mom." They hadn't shared a tender moment in quite a while. Had he been wrong about her and her display of affection toward him? It was more than they'd shared in years outside of quick greeting hugs.

The bubbly waiter returned with a contagious smile, interrupted their moment with her announcement of the daily specials, and took their orders. Pamela ordered the lobster bisque she'd heard so much about. Brian ordered shrimp scampi with a side of broccoli. They both declined the appetizers and bread and had water to drink. The waiter collected their menus and headed straight to the kitchen to submit their orders.

"So, what's her name? I don't think you told me."

"Melanie."

Pamela nodded slowly and sipped her water.

"So, what's for Christmas dinner?"

"The usual: mustard greens, turkey, ham, yams, dressing, mac 'n' cheese, apple pie, and German chocolate cake. Do you have any special requests? Is there something you'd like me to prepare for your lady friend?"

"That sounds good. I don't think you need to go out of your way to make anything else." He'd learned Melanie's favorite foods and wanted to be the one to prepare them for her, not his mom. He wasn't sure why his mom insisted on preparing so much food. She and his dad both only had one other sibling, and his dad's brother lived in Georgia. Her sister and family would probably stop by, but even if they did, she still cooked too much food for such a small crowd, creating leftovers for days. His dad didn't mind, but Brian did. Growing up, he was glad to only see turkey and ham for Thanksgiving and Christmas because the leftovers were endless.

"Then we're all set." Pamela's excitement escalated by the second and she pressed prayer hands against her lips. "I'll run to the store and pick up a stocking for her. I don't want her to feel left out when we do our traditional present swapping and pulling out trinkets from the stockings."

"Thanks for being open, Mom. I know this is a family holiday, and Melanie is new in my life. I don't want—"

"Nonsense. I know you well enough to know you wouldn't invite just anyone over. She must be special if she was able to knock the dust off your heart! The fact that you're even considering having her spend the holidays with us says enough. Don't worry about a thing. You know I don't mind entertaining, and I'm sure your dad is okay with it. Just bring the woman." She waved her hand and encouraged him with a wink.

The waiter arrived and announced their orders. He balanced the serving tray on his shoulder like he'd been doing so for years, removed their entrees and set the plates on the table before them, along with the announcement, *"hot plate."*

"Enjoy." He tossed over his shoulder and left as quickly as he arrived.

Brian reached across the table, took his mother's hand, and said a prayer of thanks.

"Amen," they said in unison.

Brian's anticipation of Christmas grew with each passing moment. Were his prayers being answered about his tattered relationship with his mother? Lately, she'd been gentler and warmer than she had been in the past.

Could this Christmas be one he'd hold close to his heart for the rest of his life—a Christmas where he repaired his relationship with his mother and swept Melanie off her feet?

Chapter 8

"Hey, boss." Shane McDaniels called out to Brian when he walked in the precinct.

"What's up, McDaniels? What's been going on, man?" Brian shook Shane's hand and gave him a one-arm hug and slap on the back.

"I have a proposition for you." Shane pulled Brian to the side out of earshot of anyone passing by. They stood just inside the break room where Shane could see if anyone was coming in or out. "I'm thinking of starting my own private detective agency, and it would be smart to have a partner, someone I already work well with." Shane grinned and slapped Brian's shoulder with his fist.

"I wasn't expecting to hear that this morning."

Shane leaned against the doorjamb and folded his arms across his chest. "C'mon. Just think about it. Mull it over. I'm not asking for an answer today or even this week. Take your time. I think we can do well. I mean, you're great at what you do, and we'd get to choose the type of cases we take. You can't tell me you like working homicide cases all the time. That's got to be getting old for you." Shane pleaded his case.

Brian smoothed the stubble on his chin and contemplated Shane's proposal. "You've got a point there. Are you saying you don't like working in property crimes? I thought you transferred because you got tired of working with me here in homicide. Wasn't I working you too hard?"

Shane angled his head back and chuckled. "Yeah, I had to leave you so Chloe wouldn't get confused about my loyalty."

Brian's shoulders shook and a hearty chuckle followed. "And yet here you are."

"Alright, man. Let's get serious. Give it some thought."

Brian folded his arms across his chest, mirroring Shane's stance. "We'd be giving up retirement and medical benefits."

"I didn't say there wasn't any risk. Just something I've been thinking about. I haven't quite talked it over with Chloe just yet and haven't got a plan either. I had a dream about it a couple of times, and both times, you were working alongside me." Shane nodded at Brian with an I'm-talking-about-you kind of smirk.

"Is that right?" Brian raised an eyebrow, and his voice held a bit of skepticism.

"Yeah, man. Just think about it, and we'll talk soon. I'm heading out, so I'll catch you later." Shane patted Brian's shoulder on the way out the door.

Since he'd already been ushered into the break room, Brian brewed a cup of coffee in the new Keurig. It had taken forever for them to get one of those with the authorities claiming that was a luxury item and not in the budget. He brewed his usual morning roast while his wheels turned thinking of Shane's proposal. It wasn't a bad idea, just something he thought he'd do once he retired, not quit to do in the middle of his career.

He grabbed his cup, added a spoonful of creamer, went to his desk, and powered on his laptop. He skimmed the unopened e-mails by sender and subject, determining which ones he would read. He found many of the e-mails he received didn't have much to do with him, so he didn't waste too much time reading them. His phone vibrated, and he pulled it out of the belt clip to check the message. Melanie.

Good morning, Brian. Just wanted to wish you a blessed day.

She was all he thought about—ways to spend time with her without seeming weird or desperate. He usually reached out to her first, but this morning had been full of surprises. First, a flat tire, then Shane's proposal.

Good morning, Melanie. Can I stop by your shop to see you today?

Sure. Around noon is good.

Great. I'll see you then. And you have a blessed day too.

☺

Melanie took up permanent space in his mind. If he could speed up the time, he would do so to see her sooner rather than later. With a schedule as unpredictable as his, Shane's offer became more attractive. That would allow him the flexibility to see more of her instead of the way he got to see her nowadays, in spurts, like he had to steal time here and there. He could be jumping the gun when it came to the longevity of their relationship, but it was important for him to be properly positioned and show Melanie he prioritized their relationship. He made a mental note to add Shane's proposal to his prayer list. He'd pray and allow God to lead Him because if he continued to mull over it, all he'd do is make a mess of the situation, both with Melanie and the career shift.

Brian turned his attention to his computer screen to regain his focus on the ongoing case of the woman murdered in Whitfield Estates. He read through the notes of the autopsy report. She was strangled then shot, which supported his theory she knew her attacker. He buzzed the new detective who'd been assigned to work alongside him, Clyde Farrington.

"It's Morris. Have you looked at the autopsy report for Ms. Gibson?"

"Mornin,' Morris. Not yet."

"Take a few minutes to look it over. We're gonna go pay our bartender friend another visit. My gut tells me he knows more than he shared the last time we spoke to him."

"Will do. See you in a bit."

Brian pulled the file from his drawer, reviewed the pictures from the crime scene, while questions formulated in his mind. He checked his notepad for the bartender's name and Googled him to get a hit on the bar where he worked. Perhaps Ms. Gibson had been to the bar and other workers would recognize her. He jotted down the name and address of the bar and reviewed a few pictures that appeared on social media. He surfed through pictures for about ten minutes before he came across a picture of the bartender neighbor and Ms. Gibson together in the bar. He'd given Brian the impression he only knew the victim as a neighbor, but judging from the closeness they shared in the photo, they appeared to be much more acquainted than neighbors who'd wave hello and goodbye from time to time.

As planned, Brian and Farrington visited the bartender at his home, rapped on the door, and announced themselves.

"Mark, it's Detectives Morris and Farrington. We'd like to ask you a few more questions about Ms. Brittany Gibson." After a minute of no response, Brian knocked on the door, rang the doorbell, and repeated himself while Farrington took notice of the exterior of the home: The one-story brown-and-red brick home with cheaply installed blinds, cracked cemented porch, rickety wood gate, and poor landscaping with more weeds than plants seemed out of place in the neighborhood compared to the rest of the two-story homes with updated entry doors, beautiful landscaping, and wrought-iron gates.

Mark opened the door in a white t-shirt and blue striped pajama pants, rubbed his eyes, and cleared his throat. Groggily, he said, "Hi. Sorry. How can I help y'all today?"

"We have a few more questions for you. Is it alright if we come in?" Brian asked.

"*Ummm,* sure. I don't really have anything else to add other than what I've already told you last time," Mark said through a yawn and stepped aside to allow Brian and Farrington inside. "Excuse me. My schedule is a bit different from yours. I'm awake at night and sleep during the day."

Brian noted the last time they spoke, Mark mentioned he was asleep when he heard the disturbance. Brian nodded. "How many nights do you work a week?"

"Five. Wednesdays through Sundays. We're closed on Mondays and Tuesdays." Mark yawned again. "Excuse me."

"Tell me about the Monday night Ms. Brittany Gibson died. Did you work the night before?"

"Sorry. My brain is fuzzy. You know how that is when someone wakes you up in the middle of your sleep, right? Let me get my thoughts together for a sec." He paused and squeezed his eyes shut like the answer would come from behind his lids. He continued, "As usual, I went to work. I saw her at the bar that night. She'd been drinking with a few friends. I saw her with some dude—someone I hadn't seen in the bar before. If he had been there, I didn't recognize him. Tall, dark, thick beard, and weird glasses. That's all I remember about him. He wasn't drinking, only flirting with her really. She seemed to be getting a kick out of it, but I'm not sure anything came of the flirting because she didn't leave with him."

"Do you know who she left with?" Farrington interjected.

Mark squeezed his eyes shut again like he searched for answers. "*Uhhh,* I don't remember. I could ask Jackson. He worked with me that night. He may remember, but I can't think of who it could have been right now. Maybe her girlfriends. She was good about leaving with who she came with. But who's to say for sure? It was busy in the bar that night. The game was on. Memphis Grizzlies were playing."

"Do you know the names of her girlfriends?" Farrington took the opportunity to jump in again.

"Nah. Sorry. I don't."

Brian leaned forward; his elbows rested on his knees. His glare could have burned a hole in Mark's skull. "Tell us about your relationship with her."

Mark's eyes enlarged wider than they had been the entire time. He avoided eye contact and cracked his knuckles. "We're neighbors really. We've gone out a few times, nothing too serious. I don't think I was ever really her type. Not really sure she could have seen herself with a bartender for the long-term."

"How many times did you go out?" Brian asked pointedly.

"Five or six times, maybe."

"And when was the last time you two went out?"

"I don't mean any harm, detective, but I need to get back to sleep because I have to work tonight, and I don't see how me going out with her has anything to do with what happened to her."

"We'll get out of your hair in a moment, but it helps us to know what kind of relationship you had with the victim. Did you love her?" Brian continued his line of questioning.

Mark rubbed his palms along the side of his face and rested his head against the back of the worn-down sofa. "Like I said, we only went out a few times."

Brian glared at Mark but kept his tone even and professional. Didn't Mark know he'd been doing this job long enough to know when someone was lying to him? "How long have you known her?"

Mark closed his eyes and maintained his position on the sofa. "I've been here about a year or so now, so at least that long."

"Thanks for your time today, Mark. We'll let you get back to your rest now." Both detectives stood, extended a handshake to Mark, and let themselves out with Mark locking the door behind them.

"I'm almost certain he's our guy," Brian said to Farrington once they were back inside of the unmarked cruiser.

"How do you know?"

Brian started the car and ticked off his reasoning on his right hand. "He has motive. He was clearly in love with her, and she didn't love him back. Became jealous when she flirted with new guy in the bar and that tipped him over the edge. They had dinner, he confronted her, and things got out of control. Did you notice his right-hand trembling?"

"Yeah, I did."

"And eyes twitching, which he tried to hide by squeezing them shut? Now that could have been the sleep, but I doubt it. He's our guy. We just have to find proof."

Brian and Farrington discussed next steps on the way back to the precinct. When they arrived, he switched the gearshift into park to allow Farrington out of the car and to text Melanie about lunch plans. She had to move a client's schedule up so she wouldn't be able to leave for lunch with him like she had originally planned.

Improvise.

He would take however many minutes he could get to erase the imagery of Mark's bloodshot eyes with that of the almond-colored eyes of the woman who was quickly taking hold of his heart.

Chapter 9

How could he make the most of their abbreviated time together? Brian thought back to the conversation they'd had about favorite foods, called in a to-go order of boudin and sweet tea from the Seafood Kitchen, and picked up their lunch en route to the salon.

The spices wafted through the car, tickling his nostrils, and teasing his stomach. This would be his first time trying boudin, and from the smell of it, Melanie had great taste. He didn't waste any time when he arrived at the salon, whipping into the first parking space he saw. He zipped up his jacket and slipped on a knit cap before he braved the cool air, something he hadn't done all morning.

The first time he walked through the building handing out flyers, the maze of hallways had him a bit confused, but walking into Melanie's booth was unforgettable. Without the need to look for any signage, he found his way back to her booth by memory, seasoned boudin accompanying him.

Brian tapped on the door and waited for Melanie's "come in" to gain entry.

"Hey! You're right on time. My last client just walked out the door." Melanie hugged him when he entered.

"I was hoping I would be. It's so good to see your sweet face." Brian rubbed the back of his palm along her cheek and held her gaze longer than he intended, but her eyes had a way of pulling him in. He swallowed the knot that formed at the base of his throat and lowered his eyes to her lips. Melanie's I'm-happy-to-see-you smile sent his emotions spiraling out of control in a matter of seconds.

Brian put space in between them and held the bag of food in the air.

"Oh, that smells so good. Tell me that is not what I think it is." Melanie's voice raised an octave in excitement.

"Well, if you were thinking boudin, then that's exactly what you think it is." Brian proudly opened the bag and handed her the contents. "I got some for me, too. I hope it's as good as you said."

"Thanks, Brian. I didn't have anything but two boiled eggs and a piece of toast this morning." Melanie patted her belly. "I'm starving."

"I'm glad I could be of service to you, then."

"Sorry I had to change our plans. My client is going out of town and needed to change her appointment. Thanks for being understanding." Melanie apologized and opened the Styrofoam container. She inhaled the aroma and smiled. "Oh, this is about to be so good."

Brian was proud of himself for showing he'd listened to her and acted on it. Judging from her reaction, he pleased her, and that's what he desired to do, fill her life with goodness and joy.

"Let's pray." Brian reached for her free hand. "Father God, we love and honor You on today. Thank You for allowing us this time together. Please bless Melanie and guide her throughout the rest of her day. We thank You for our food and ask that You bless it to nourish our bodies. In Jesus' name. Amen."

"Amen."

Melanie sat in the salon chair while Brian took a seat across from her in the dryer chair. She started eating her boudin with a fork but paused to wait for Brian's initial reaction. His eyebrows shot up in delight.

"Good, right?"

"Yes. This has to be the best Cajun rice I've tasted."

"I know. I first tried these when I visited my aunt one year in Houston. I searched high and low for a local restaurant to get my fill of them. It's not something I can eat too often because of the spices and calories, but the calories are well worth it when I do indulge." Melanie took another bite.

Brian didn't seem to mind the spice given he scoffed his portion down in about ten minutes.

"How's your day going so far?"

"Pretty good. Any day where work is steady is a good day. The smile on your face tells me you're having a rather good day too," Melanie said in between bites.

"We went out to follow a lead this morning, and I think we may have enough information to build on, and that's always a good thing. I can't stop people from hurting others, but if I can give the victim's family closure and justice, I've done my job. But this smile has nothing to do with work. It's all you." Brian winked and his I-can't-get-enough-of-you-smile broadened.

Melanie held his gaze for a few seconds, twisted and chewed her bottom lip before she finally met his smile with her own.

"Thank you." Melanie stuffed a forkful of food in her mouth.

"Are we still on for Christmas dinner? Say yes because I already told my mom you were coming."

Melanie leaned back in her seat and raised an eyebrow. "So, you told your mom about me?"

His eyes widened and his eyebrows shot up. "Of course, I did." Then Brian's eyes narrowed, and he licked his lips. His gaze steady and his voice gentle, but firm. "In case you haven't figured it out by now, you're special to me, Melanie, and I hope to have you in my life for a long time."

Melanie placed a hand over her heart. "You're special to me, too," she admitted, her voice lighter and sweeter.

Brian's chest tightened and he eased the tension with the ball of his hand. What was it about her that made him want to give her the best part of him?

Tap. Tap. Melanie's salon door opened. "I'm on time today, Mel," Charise announced when she walked through the door. Her jaw dropped at the sight of Brian. She then twisted her lips with an "*Ummm*."

"It's okay. Come on in. I'm getting ready to leave." Brian chuckled at Charise's reaction as he stood. He gathered the empty containers and placed them in the same plastic bag he'd brought them in.

"Let me walk you out. Give me one minute, Charise," Melanie called over her shoulder and closed the door behind her after she stepped in the hallway. "Thanks for coming to see me. Since I had to change our plans a bit, let me make it up to you."

"How about lunch after you join me for church on Sunday?"

"Sounds good to me."

"I'll call you later," Brian promised and embraced her, the mold of her body perfect in his arms. Did she snuggle closer?

"Have a good rest of the day."

"Thanks, Brian. You, too."

∞

Melanie relished being in Brian's arms, her heart raced by the second. The same rush of electricity she experienced the first time he touched her hand now pulsed in the left section of her chest. Brian's hugs brought security about the future and told her that everything would be alright. What would her therapist think about it? Would she think she was moving too fast? Grasping on to Brian because he was now the constant in her life and made her feel safe? No matter what her thoughts were, Melanie wanted Brian to stick around.

"Don't say a word," Melanie commanded when she was back inside her salon studio.

"What?"

"Charise, you started when you first came in here." Melanie motioned for her to sit at the shampoo bowl.

"I didn't say anything, but if you want to say something, my ears are open. I told you I look forward to coming to see you. You're my escape. I find out new things and learn what's going on in the world while I'm in your chair." Charise rested her head in the curve of the shampoo bowl, rhythmically raising her eyebrows up and down.

"I bet you do."

Melanie trusted Charise. Over the years, they'd shared many stories with one another. In fact, Charise was the only client she'd shared any deeply personal information with and not crossed any boundaries. They met while they were college roommates freshman year at Tennessee State University, both English majors. Over the first semester, their dorm room slowly became a hair salon with Melanie rolling, wrapping, cutting, coloring, and braiding hair for twenty dollars. She was often complimented on her skill and soon realized her passion for cosmetology was greater than that of English literature. At the end of the first semester, she didn't return to Tennessee State University.

During that Christmas break, she enrolled in cosmetology school, a move her parents didn't support initially. When she finished, she came back home to Nashville and opened her shop. Charise came home to support her and be her first customer. Their friendship remained solid over time with them supporting each other through Charise's dating, engagement, marriage, and motherhood and Melanie's cosmetology career, broken relationships, death of her parents in a car crash, and recently through the death of her friend Natalie.

"That's the detective that came in with that flyer after Thanksgiving, right?"

"Yes, ma'am."

"Come on, Mel. Don't make me pull your teeth to get the tea." She opened her eyes to see Melanie hovering over her with the water sprayer. "That smile on your face tells me you have news to share. What gives?"

"*Ummm*…not really sure what to say. I do like him, and we've been having an enjoyable time together. It doesn't hurt that he's easy on the eyes. He's spiritual too. I'm going to church with him on Sunday. I'd have to say I do think this is the first time I've been invited to church by a guy."

"I like it. Sounds good. I can tell he's head over heels for you, too."

"How so?" Melanie massaged shampoo throughout Charise's hair.

"Honey, I knew the moment he stepped in here with that flyer. He's one of those guys who wears his heart on his sleeve, his bulging sleeve, might I add." Charise jabbed a finger in the air. "It's hard for him to mask emotion. Plus, if I didn't know then, I knew it the moment I walked in here a while ago. I saw all thirty-two of his teeth this time. Or was it thirty-three? What did you say to him? You'd let him protect and serve you?"

"Charise, you're so nosy." Melanie chuckled, rinsed out the shampoo and massaged conditioner throughout Charise's long locks.

"Call me what you want, but you can't call me wrong. I just call it like I see it. He was in here smiling like you agreed to marry him."

"Okay, now you're just being ridiculous. Fishing is what you're doing. Slick is one thing you are not, chile." Melanie wagged a finger at her before wrapping her hair in a towel.

Charise walked over to the styling chair, plopped down, and continued. "Okay, so just tell me what you said or did that had him smiling like he won the lottery, and I'll leave it alone. Promise." Charise crossed her fingers.

"Nothing, actually. We were just agreeing on our next date."

"I love it. I'm so happy for you, girl. You deserve all the happiness in the world. I'm cheering for you and Mr. Handsome, girlfriend."

That made two of them.

Brian made Melanie's day a little brighter, but she refrained from mirroring his sentiment earlier. Would she have sounded insincere if she told him her smile had everything to do with him? To look at him and not think back to the day she lost Natalie was a huge step. And to believe that she deserved the happiness she experienced with him in her life was an even bigger accomplishment. So, when Brian adjusted to the change in plans, her heart pitter-pattered to a rhythm only his presence brought about.

Melanie pushed down the excitement that welled within her. She wanted things to work out between her and Brian more than anybody because she needed this win. Within the past few years, she'd lost so much—her parents, Natalie, hope. Brian could be her rainbow after the storm—at least she longed for that to be true.

Though it had only been a short time, he had grown on her in such a way that made her picture him in her life permanently.

Chapter 10

St. John Missionary Baptist Church had been Brian's church home for the last ten years. Even though he had a hectic work schedule from time to time, he took the time to be in his Father's house on Sundays, serving as a greeter when he could. With Melanie as his guest this Sunday, he volunteered for the first service only and waited for her to meet him for the later service. He'd dressed more formally today with a suit jacket and tie than he normally did, wanting to look nice for her.

He stood outside on the stairs that led up to the entrance and waited for Melanie to arrive at their agreed upon time, 10:45 a.m. He took notice of her ascending the steps in a green sheath dress, matching pumps, and a black pea coat. Brian quickly descended the steps to assist her.

"Good morning," Brian greeted her with an appreciative smile, extending an arm for her to steady herself as she continued to the entrance. "You look beautiful this morning."

"Thank you, Brian. So do you."

Though he didn't doubt her sincerity, he couldn't help but notice she seemed uncomfortable when she returned the compliment, her voice muffled and softer than usual, but he didn't address it.

"We have fresh coffee, fruit, and doughnuts at the hospitality table. Would you like to stop by before service?" Brian offered.

Melanie checked her watch and asked, "What time does service start? Do I have enough time?"

"About fifteen minutes. I can get an usher to save seats for us, so you don't have to worry about that, if that's your concern."

"Okay, then. I'll take *one* doughnut and a cup of coffee."

Brian stopped at the sanctuary entrance and whispered into an older gentleman's ear before he escorted her to the hospitality room and served her coffee with sugar and cream, along with one cake doughnut. She thanked him and took one bite and a sip of coffee. Her lips curled in delight, and she squeezed her eyes shut for a second.

"I love the combination of coffee and cake donuts."

"I think everyone around us knows," Brian teased. "C'mon, let me introduce you to a few people."

He took her around the room and introduced her to the leader of the women's ministry, Rebecca Stanton; the prayer team leader, Steven Foster; and one of his closest friends, Jeremiah Woods. Afterward, he led her to an empty table to finish her refreshments.

"Brian, son, how are you?" Pastor Davidson approached the table in his black pulpit robe. Their church wasn't small, but it wasn't one of those mega churches either. Melanie was the first woman he'd brought to church since his breakup with Penelope. One of the most eligible bachelors, the word had probably gotten out Brian had a woman with him this morning, hence the reason Pastor Davidson approached him, something he hardly ever did before service.

"I'm great, Pastor. How are you? This is Melanie. Melanie, this is Pastor Davidson."

"Nice to meet you, sir." Melanie shook his extended hand.

"It's a pleasure to meet you too, young lady." He smiled and peered over his bifocals from Melanie to Brian. "I hope you enjoy the service and come back to see us again sometime."

"Thank you."

"Brian, thank you for serving this morning. Appreciate you, son." Pastor Davidson patted him on the back and left the room to take his seat in the pulpit, the scent of his cologne hung around like the third wheel.

"Friendly members," Melanie commented after she swallowed another piece of doughnut and washed it down with a sip of coffee.

Brian slid his white folding chair an inch closer to Melanie and rested his forearms on the table. "We try to be. Don't want to turn anyone away by being ugly. So many people don't attend church today because of how another parishioner treated them. That is one thing Pastor preaches about and doesn't want to be said of this church."

"I see. Is this your parents' church too?" Melanie's eyes darted around the room like she expected to see them any minute.

"No. They go to church across town—Pilgrim's Rest. I grew up there but changed my membership here about ten years ago."

Brian took note of the rise and fall in Melanie's chest. She agreed to join him for Christmas dinner, but had she changed her mind? Did the thought of meeting his parents give her pause? Was she concerned their relationship was progressing too quickly?

He flipped his wrist to check the time. "Service is starting in two minutes. Are you ready to head into the sanctuary?"

"Sure." Melanie downed the rest of her coffee.

Brian took the napkin and empty cup to the trash and escorted her into the sanctuary. He instinctively reached for her hand but quickly dropped his hand to his side. He didn't want to make her uncomfortable nor stir up any rumors. If he'd held her hand, he would be married off by next Sunday in someone's mind. Instead, he leaned over, whispered to follow him, and escorted her to the seats an usher reserved for him at the end of the third row— close enough to the front to avoid distraction.

Two minutes after they took their seat, they were encouraged to stand again to join the choir in praise. Melanie's voice caught Brian by surprise, and the fact she knew most of the lyrics. By the time Pastor Davidson approached the microphone, her face was stained with tears. Brian handed her a tissue, which she quickly accepted. After Pastor Davidson read the focal Scripture, the congregation took their seats, and he began to preach.

Melanie took notes and followed along with the message, "I Just Can't Give Up Now."

"Take Moses for example. He went to pharaoh ten times to tell him God said to let His people go. After the third no, most of us would have given up, but Moses kept going. I imagine he was getting weary, but he trusted God. Write this down: When the enemy fights back, I must fight even harder. See, church, the enemy doesn't want your things. He doesn't want your job, your house, your car, or any other material thing you can think of. He wants your faith. If he can get you to give up and live a defeated life, then he's won. But Jesus came so you may have life and have it more abundantly. Amen?"

"Amen," the congregation agreed as Pastor Davidson continued.

∞

If Melanie hadn't known any better, she'd think Pastor Davidson had been spying on her life, but she knew better. It wasn't an accident she was present that morning. Every word of that sermon was for her and she received the message not to give up. She took as many notes as she could throughout the rest of his sermon with asterisks, underlines, and caps.

When service ended, she joined Brian at the altar for prayer. She enjoyed service today more than she did at her home church and would be happy to join Brian again at his next invitation.

Brian accompanied Melanie to the hospitality room once again at the end of service. First-time visitors met with Pastor Davidson after church, where he shook each one of their hands and gave them a gift bag filled with a copy of the earlier morning's sermon, an *Our Daily Bread* devotional, and a cup, pen, and hand sanitizer with the church's logo.

"We are blessed you chose to visit with us today. Are there any questions I can answer for anyone about our church?" Pastor Davidson asked to which everyone shook their heads.

"I know it's lunchtime. I'll let you all go but let me pray for you first. Heavenly Father, thank You for Your mercies and grace that are new each morning. Forgive us our sins as we forgive those who have sinned against us. Lord, we humbly come to thank You for who You are in our lives and ask that You watch over Your sons and daughters this week, leading them in the paths of righteousness for Your name's sake. Guide them, protect them, and allow them to see You in ways they haven't seen You before this week. Where they have questions, give them answers. Let Your love and light rule their hearts. Allow them to see You beyond all else. In Jesus' holy name we pray. Amen."

"Amen," the visitors sang in agreement, then shook Pastor Davidson's hand one last time as they exited the room.

Melanie and Brian were at the end of the line. Pastor Davidson clasped Melanie's hand and squinted. "May God bless you, Melanie, and grant you the desires of your heart."

"Thank you, Pastor Davidson."

Pastor Davidson clutched Brian's hands. "Thank you for inviting Melanie to worship with us today. I hope we'll be seeing more of her."

"Thanks, Pastor. See you next week."

∞

Brian escorted her out of the room and building, but this time he held her hand as she descended the steps. Her hand trembled a bit at his touch and he secured his grasp, the connection increased the speed of his pulse.

Could she feel it through his fingertips?

"What did you think of our service?" Brian led her through the parking lot.

"Refreshing." Melanie glanced heavenward, inhaled, and exhaled deeply. "Very refreshing, and the sermon was timely."

"I hope that means you'll come again." Brian paused briefly in the middle of the parking lot, squeezed her hand, and searched her eyes like he'd asked her a more serious question.

"If I'm invited." Melanie flashed an I'll-go-anywhere-you-invite-me kind of smile.

"Consider this your invitation." He kissed the top of her head and cleared his throat. "So, lunch. Where to?"

"You choose. This is me making it up to you because I had to cancel our date earlier in the week, remember? What do you have a taste for eating?"

"Soul food sounds good." Brian walked Melanie to her car. The parking lot had mostly cleared since they stayed behind to meet with Pastor Davidson. They were parked near each other with two rows in between. He opened her door and saw her safely inside.

He settled into his car, turned on the heat and seat warmer, and smiled thinking about Melanie and their future together. Her next to him in church felt right, like it was supposed to be that way.

Her next to him every Sunday or any day for that matter felt right.

His Christmas present came early this year, wrapped in the form of Melanie.

Chapter 11

Melanie could count on one hand the number of guys' parents she'd met. She rummaged through her closet and changed out of a dress into a skirt and blouse, out of that ensemble and into a pair of jeans and sweater and back into a dress again, only to change her mind once more, which drove her insane. Making a great impression was important, and out of all the days of the year she agreed to meet his parents, it had to be Christmas Day. If this went sour, she wouldn't be able to forget the memory because she'd always associate it with Christmas, no matter how hard she would try to forget. No amount of counseling would be able to sweep the terrible memories away or help her put them behind her. She had to get her outfit together. The last thing Brian's parents would be able to say about her is that she looked terrible.

She stepped out of her walk-in closet to check the time, threw herself on the bed, and closed her eyes.

"Lord, please don't let me make a fool of myself. I think I care way too much about this guy anyway. It's only been about a month, and I'm totally losing it. Please let today go well. Amen."

Her eyes widened at the vibration underneath her. Her phone. No doubt it would be either Brian or Charise, most likely Brian. Charise should be busy with her own family today. Melanie filtered through the sheets, pulled out her phone to see Brian's name light across the screen, and swiped to answer.

"Merry Christmas again."

"Merry Christmas, Mel. I'm headed your way. I'll be there in about thirty minutes. Are you ready?"

She considered his question, and her stomach twisted in knots. An easy yes-or-no answer would suffice, so why was she overwhelmed? She couldn't cancel at the last minute. She wanted to see Brian, but was she ready to meet his parents today? Ugh, where was her therapist when she needed her? She'd know what to say to make her think about this rationally and calmly.

"*Ummm,* I'll be ready by the time you get here." She failed at masking her anxiety with a softer voice. Brian noticed she sounded less cheery. "You feelin' okay?"

"Yeah, yeah. I'm good." She waved him off like he could see her. "Let me finish up, and I'll see you when you get here."

"Alright. See you soon, Mel." Melanie could feel his smile in his voice.

"Drive safely. See you." Melanie swiped to end the call and tossed the phone back onto the bed next to her where she continued to lay.

"Okay, Lord. I'm really, really, really nervous. I know your word says not to be anxious, but I can't really help it right now." Melanie found the holiday music channel in the cable lineup and selected soothing Christmas songs to help calm her nerves while she settled on the jeans and sweater. The atmosphere should be relaxing. If Brian thought she should dress up, he would have mentioned it. She played with different palates of eyeshadow until the doorbell rang. Satisfied with her final look, Melanie made her way to the door, her chest heaved slowly but her heart was seconds away from creating a gaping hole in her chest.

"Merry Christmas!" Brian pulled her into his arms as soon as she was within sight. His avocado argyle sweater and relaxed fitting blue jeans paired nicely with her candy apple sweater and indigo skinny jeans. "I'm glad I get to spend this day with you. You're beautiful, Mel."

"Thank you, Brian. Merry Christmas." She buried her face in his neck. Her shoulders relaxed and her breathing evened. She had nothing to be anxious about, everything would be alright.

"Ready?" Brian put space in between them, and she stepped out of his arms.

"Yeah. I just need to grab my shoes, coat, and purse." Melanie invited Brian inside, turned down the volume on the traditional Christmas music that played on the TV's holiday music station, and whisked away to her bedroom to find a pair of black calf-length pointed toe boots and to grab her matching purse and peacoat off the hanger. "You got this, girl," Melanie whispered to herself on the way back into the living room where she'd left Brian waiting.

"Alright. Ready. Are you sure there isn't anything I can bring?" Melanie spread her hands wide, palms up. Worry lines etched in her forehead.

"No. My mom has probably outdone herself with the food and decorations." Brian reached for her hand.

Melanie hesitated to accept his hand, thought for a moment, and shifted from one foot to the other. She stayed up late last night searching through online recipes to bake the perfect batch of chocolate chip cookies. Call her crazy, but she wanted to make a good impression and showing up empty-handed didn't spell good manners to her. Against Brian's advice, she made a beeline for the kitchen to pack the cookies she'd prepared, tied in cellophane, and stored in a green-and-red Christmas tin she'd scored from the dollar store.

"I'll just feel better if I bring something." Melanie held up the tin can when she returned to the room.

"You're baking for me already? What did I ever do to deserve you?"

"Not you, silly." She swatted his hand away. "This is my hostess gift."

"I'm sure she'll be just as impressed as I am."

Brian reached for her hand again and she accepted. A wave of comfort enveloped her the second their hands connected. She relaxed and an everything-is-going-to-be-alright smile formed on her lips.

Nothing to worry about.

∞

Brian's anxiety was different from Melanie's. While she was nervous about meeting his parents, Brian couldn't wait to show her off. If Melanie couldn't tell he was proud of her and what was becoming of their relationship by his invitation to his church, he hoped introducing her to his parents would help solidify his thoughts and intentions toward her.

Brian pulled up to a beautiful red brick house with fresh landscaping, something Melanie didn't often see during the winter months. Brian didn't waste any time getting out of the car after turning off the engine. As he always did, he opened her door and extended an arm to steady her as she got out of the car. He held her free hand and led her along stone pavers to the front entrance.

Brian didn't bother ringing the doorbell and waiting outside as usual. He had a key to his parents' house since moving out after joining the force and could count on one hand the number of times he'd used it. This seemed a special enough occasion to do so.

"We're here," Brian called out to his parents when he and Melanie entered. The familiar scent of apple cinnamon greeted him at the door and memories of Christmas mornings as a child flooded his mind. His mouth watered because he knew there would be apple pie for dessert.

He removed his coat and helped Melanie with her coat and purse, hung them on the coat rack in the foyer and proceeded to the kitchen where he was sure to find his parents.

"Merry Christmas!"

Pamela met them in the living room, her arms spread wide. She squeezed Brian, and a wave of emotion overtook him. Was this the woman she'd always been or had the spirit of the season took over?

Melanie's smile looked like it hurt, like she'd bit down into a candy cane and damaged her tooth. Nothing like Brian had grown accustomed to.

"Merry Christmas, Mom. This is Melanie."

Pamela encircled Melanie in her arms the same way she did Brian.

"Merry Christmas, Melanie."

"Merry Christmas!" Melanie's voice cracked.

Brian rubbed his hand along Melanie's shoulder. Was it him or was she overly nervous? Brian thought back to the day he introduced Penelope to his parents. Penelope immediately inserted herself as part of his family and made nice with his mom. They'd been dating almost a year at the time.

Was it the timing?

According to Penelope, he dragged his feet when it came to his commitment in their relationship, but was he moving too fast for Melanie?

Melanie would have told him if she was uncomfortable with the idea of meeting his parents, wouldn't she? He cared about Penelope but, his emotional connection to Melanie was unmatched. Surely, he hadn't been wrong about Melanie's feelings for him.

"Well come on in. Dinner is about ready."

"Oh, these are for you." Melanie handed her the tin of homemade cookies.

Pamela peered inside. "Cookies. What kind?"

"Chocolate chip."

"One of my favorites. Did Brian tell you?" Pamela beamed and bounced her shoulders.

"No, he didn't." Melanie clasped her hands in front of her like a child waiting for their punishment. "Chocolate chip seems to be a universal favorite. I hoped you'd like them, too."

Brian briefly rubbed Melanie's shoulders and she relaxed, her smile now met her eyes.

"Love them. Thank you." Pamela reassuringly squeezed Melanie's hand. "Come meet Stanley. Honey, Brian and Melanie are here," Pamela called out and led them through the house into the kitchen. Pamela decorated far beyond dressing a Christmas tree with lights and ornaments. Green and red garland covered the spindles on the stairs. Décor pillows on the sofas were Christmas themed. Snow globes covered the fireplace mantel. Cross-adorned wreaths hung on every door. Mistletoes hung in every door opening. Both coffee tables in the living room were adorned with the nativity scene. Frankly, Brian was surprised the outside of the house wasn't covered in Christmas lights this year.

Stanley Morris stood from the table where he drank his afternoon coffee and greeted both Brian and Melanie with a bear-like hug. His parents welcomed her like she was a part of this family. And that was a thought he could get used to.

Chapter 12

"I made a little bit of everything." Pamela waved her arm across the platinum serving trays and pans to showcase her work. "Turkey, ham, mustard greens, macaroni and cheese, yams, green bean casserole, broccoli rice and cheese casserole, dressing, white rice with gravy, steamed broccoli, and butter rolls made from scratch. Melanie, since you're our guest, I'll prepare a plate for you first. What would you like, dear?"

"I'll take a little of everything," Melanie answered graciously. She didn't care for yams or either of the casseroles Pamela mentioned, but she'd try them to keep from being offensive. If Pamela were anything like her mother, she'd be offended if she invited someone into her home and they didn't at least try her cooking. She'd always say you don't know if you like it if you haven't tried it. Sure, some recipes varied, but to Melanie they were all the same. It couldn't taste much different.

"Here you go. Your place setting is right next to Brian's."

Pamela handed the plate to Melanie and eyed her closely. Melanie saw something flash in her eyes but wasn't sure what. Was she being paranoid? Was Pamela trying to communicate something to her she wasn't catching?

"Mom, I can fix my own plate. You don't have to do that." Brian motioned to get out of the seat where he sat directly across from his father.

"Son, you know it's my pleasure. Sit down." She waved him back to his seat. "I can handle it. I'll only be a few more minutes. Go ahead and enjoy your father and Melanie while I finish up." She piled food onto Brian and Stanley's plates, then prepared her own plate last and joined them at the table.

"So, Melanie, before we ask God's blessing and eat, we have a tradition where we like to say what we're thankful for this year. I know most folks only do this for Thanksgiving, but we do it for Christmas as well around here. Helps keep the focus on the gift God gave to us on Christmas—Jesus. And He's been giving to us all year. Since you're our special guest, would you like to go first?" Stanley asked.

Taken aback, Melanie thought for a moment. "*Ummm.* Sure. I'm thankful for this moment, actually. Thank you for welcoming me into your home. I'm not sure if Brian shared this with you, but my parents died several years ago in a car crash, so it's nice to be able to share in this special holiday with family."

Brian slipped one arm around her shoulder and squeezed. "We're glad to have you here with us. And with that, I'll go next. I'm thankful for God's continuous grace with me throughout each day. You know I work a lot, but He is always directing me and positioning me in the right place at just the right time. Even through tragedy, He can mend hearts and draw people together. Though my work can sometimes be a little daunting, if it weren't for that work, I don't know when or how I would have met you." He turned to Melanie. "And I'm thankful that God put you in my life."

Melanie leaned into the arm that never left her shoulder, smiled in acknowledgment, and took captive the thoughts that sought to creep up in her mind that reminded her how she met Brian – a stunning replica of his father, younger and more athletic

"This has been a blessed year for me." Pamela crossed her hands over her chest. "I could name a hundred things I'm thankful for, but I'll settle on a few: Though my daughter decided to spend Christmas elsewhere this year, she is healthy and well. I have both of my favorite guys at the table with me for Christmas without interruption of work. Melanie, work is a big deal for these men. I'm sure Brian gets his work ethic from Stanley. But looks as if he's learning to put work in its proper place." She paused and exchanged glances with Brian. "I give thanks to God for many of my clients who have experienced breakthroughs in their lives from fears, addictions, and loss. And I'm thankful that God has brought Melanie to our table." Pamela spread her hands over the table like a game show model and her lips formed a toothless smile.

Melanie's heart skipped a beat when Pamela mentioned counseling. For the life of her, she didn't know why she was bothered if Brian found out anyway. Was it the stigma attached to the idea of people seeking mental health treatment? Seeking help was normal—now her normal.

If she had done so after her parents died, she would have been better off for it, but the loss of Natalie somehow tipped her over the edge, especially since she was present at the time of her murder.

"I'm thankful for life," Stanley began. "I'm thankful for the love of family and friends and for God's love for me. He loved me enough to send Baby Jesus to this earth, and for that, I say thank ya, Lord. Let us pray: Father God, thank You for Your gift of Jesus Christ to this world. Thank You for loving us so much that You would give up Your only son for our sake. Father God, help us to remember what this day is about. The presents are good, but it isn't about them, but about Your present to us: Jesus. Thank You for family gathered here today. We pray the words of our mouths and the meditation of our hearts be acceptable in Your sight. We pray and ask that You lead us in the paths of righteousness for Your name's sake. We pray and thank You for Your goodness and mercy and ask that You help us to keep You first in all that we do and seek to do. We ask that You bless our food for the nourishment of our bodies and that You bless our cook who had the will and desire to serve us today. Thank You for her heart to serve. In Jesus' name. Amen."

"Amen," they all said in agreement.

"Fooling around with y'all and these speeches, my food is going to be cold," Stanley joked.

Melanie, Brian, and Stanley praised Pamela for each dish they tasted. She smiled warmly and graciously accepted their gratitude. Melanie watched her. The woman who sat before her seemed warm and caring, gentle, and nurturing.

"So, tell us about yourself, Melanie," Pamela said. "What do you do for a living?"

"I have a salon studio in Salon Park off Main Street. Work is steady, but I still have flexibility, which I like."

"You're a cosmetologist?" Stanley questioned and stuffed a forkful of dressing into his mouth.

"Oh, yes I didn't mention that, did I? After one semester in college, I found my calling on the fifth floor of Mary Wilson Hall at Tennessee State University." She chuckled a bit recalling the memory. "After Christmas break, I didn't go back. I decided to enroll in cosmetology school, so I've been a stylist for about fifteen years now."

Stanley washed down a healthy serving of cornbread dressing with his glass of water. "Good for you."

"Brian tells me you're an accountant, right?"

"Thirty-five years. You probably automatically think taxes or bookkeeping, but I'm an auditor at one of the Big Four accounting firms." He used air quotes to emphasize *Big Four*.

"Big Four?"

"Yes. Before the fall of Enron and Arthur Andersen, and before a few mergers, there were seven, so we're one of the largest accounting firms left. I started as a staff accountant right out of college with the intent to only work for a couple of years just to get enough experience to make myself more marketable for industry, but I never left. I've been a partner for the last fifteen years."

"I take it you're not going anywhere?" Melanie joked, to which Stanley joined her in a chuckle.

"No. I'll retire soon so I can live out the rest of my days enjoying life with Pam. I guess I'll work full-time for her until she gets tired of me."

"*Awww,* hush. One taste of retirement, and you won't even be thinking about work."

"What about you, Mrs. Morris? What do you do? Are you thinking of retiring soon?" Melanie asked.

"I have a while longer before I call it quits. I've only had my own private therapy practice about ten years, and I enjoy what I do. Maybe I'll bring in another associate and move to part-time so I can travel with Stanley." She wriggled her eyebrows at her husband.

"And son, what about you? Things alright at work?" Pamela pulled Brian into the conversation.

"The usual for me. Nothing new to report, really."

"Okay. We're off work today, so I don't want to talk anymore about it. If you all want to wait for dessert, we can open presents when you finish up dinner." She touched Melanie's shoulder. "Christmas stockings are another tradition we have around here, Melanie, and don't worry. Since I knew you were coming, I got one for you, too."

Still chewing his food, Brian turned to smile at her. Melanie's feelings of doubt and anxiety had faded and were replaced with sincere gratitude. Overcome with emotion, a lone tear escaped her eye, which she instantly wiped away with the back of her hand. She wasn't sure what to expect when she accepted Brian's invitation to meet his parents on an important holiday like Christmas, which she had grown to believe was meant to be shared with family.

And family was exactly how they treated her.

Chapter 13

Melanie followed Brian's lead into the festively decorated living room and sat next to him on the oversized loveseat. She carefully removed two of the reindeer-themed throw pillows and handed them to Brian instead of tossing them to the other sofa like she would have done if she were home. She rocked gently and grinned like a kid on Christmas morning while she waited for Pamela to lead the next activity.

"You okay?"

"Yeah. Kinda looking forward to what's next. Your mom's excitement is a bit contagious." Melanie nodded in Pamela's direction. "Look at her."

Pamela shimmied into the family room where she'd started the gas fireplace, called to Alexa to play her favorite Christmas music, and removed the stockings that hung along the mantel, passed one to Stanley, Brian, and Melanie and then sat next to Stanley.

Melanie dabbed at the tears that leaked from her eyes, trying hard to contain her emotion. She watched Brian and Stanley open their stockings filled with their favorite snacking nuts, candy bars, and a special gift. For Brian, two pairs of engraved cufflinks along with a gift card to Landry's, and for Stanley, a new gold fitness tracker watch and a gift card to his favorite coffee shop.

"Thanks for the gifts, Mom." Brian leaned against Melanie and nudged her shoulder with his. "Mel, open yours."

Melanie reached inside of her snowwoman-decorated stocking and felt around for a moment before pulling out two candy bars. She fancied any chocolate bar that contained nuts. She reached inside again and pulled out an Amazon gift card and immediately thought about the books that were on her wish list. The last item she pulled out was a miniature keepsake wooden jewelry box with the words *Merry Christmas* engraved on top.

"This is beautiful. Thank you." She would have liked to hug Pamela but something about it felt awkward.

"You're welcome. It's my pleasure to put smiles on your faces during this time of the year. And Melanie, it really is my pleasure to have you as a guest in our home. Now," Pamela stood and clapped her hands, "are we ready for dessert or —"

"Hold on a second, Mom. The thought you put into our family celebration every year doesn't go unnoticed. Dad, Sharice, and I love you." He walked to the Christmas tree, removed a large box, and handed it to her. "A gift from all of us."

Pamela's eyes widened and misted after she ripped through the crimson wrapping paper, opened the box, and revealed a leather designer bag.

"Now you all really didn't have to do this, but I'm glad you did." She put the bag on her shoulder, strutted, twirled around the living room, and posed like a QVC model.

Melanie sat entertained by Pamela.

"And there's one more thing." Brian pulled out his phone and video called his sister, Sharice, who answered immediately. Did the phone ring?

"Merry Christmas, Mom. I love you!" Sharice shouted over the chatter in her background.

"Merry Christmas, Sharice. I miss you. Are you enjoying yourself?" Pamela's smile widened more than it had all afternoon. Her voice rose several octaves to match her daughter's.

"Yes, Mom. All good here. Brian, where's Melanie? Let me see her."

Melanie flashed a teeth-chattering smile. Brian had only mentioned his sister a couple of times. Why was she surprised he told her about their relationship? Her mind churned at the revelation.

His intentions were genuine, not that she ever doubted they were.

"Hi Sharice. It's nice to meet you." Melanie waved at the woman who looked like the feminine version of Brian, with makeup and a full head of shiny ebony curls.

"Same here. I hope to meet you in person the next time I'm in town. Brian," Sharice yelled, and he moved the phone to look at her. "She's beautiful. Good for you, big brother. It's about time you dusted the cobwebs off your heart."

Brian shot her a playful warning glare with a raised eyebrow. "Don't start."

"Okay, I won't *this* time." She winked. "Now show me Dad."

Brian handed the phone to his dad to finish the conversation with Sharice before she rejoined her boyfriend's family.

Pamela excused herself to put her purse away. When she returned, she took dessert requests.

"I'll take a slice of German chocolate cake and apple pie, Mom," Brian called out while he gathered wrapping paper and empty gift boxes to toss in the recycle bin.

"Same here with a cup of coffee," Stanley added. "Thanks, dear."

"Melanie, why don't you come help me with the desserts in the kitchen?"

When they walked into the kitchen, out of earshot of Brian and Stanley, Pamela smiled politely and asked her to sit. Pamela's tone was different. It no longer sounded like the gentle, kind, nurturing, and adoring woman who handed out gifts moments ago.

Beads of perspiration gathered at the nape of Melanie's neck. The only thing comforting her was the aroma of freshly baked goods.

Pamela sliced German chocolate cake and poured coffee for the two of them and took a seat across from Melanie.

"I've been watching you just as much as you've been watching me, and I know this must be awkward for you. Am I right?"

Melanie took a sip a coffee and answered, "Very much so. Is this awkward for you, too? Did you know Brian would be bringing me?"

"Well, first, my professional and personal life are separate. I never share who I'm seeing or what we discuss. Nothing has changed since the first time we met. Everything you share with me stays in that office. At home, I'm a mother and a wife, and I like to keep it that way, although my family thinks I try to fix them. But who couldn't use a little fixing?" Pamela shimmied and winked. Her voice was soft and calm, the same way it was when Melanie laid on her couch and poured out her thoughts and concerns.

Melanie and Pamela shared a little laugh.

"As for Brian bringing you, I didn't know. When he mentioned your name, I thought it could be you given the way he described you, but I didn't ask too many questions. He's not a detective by accident; my son is perceptive and would have become suspicious if I dug too deep. But let me just say I'm glad it's you. You're a bright young woman, Melanie. Don't allow what you've been through to stop you from experiencing love and happiness. Oops, there I go." She motioned to remove a hat off her head.

"Thank you. I try to remember that every day."

"Just relax and enjoy yourself. Today is about love and family. Try not to think of me as your therapist. Don't forget we have lives too. We don't sit around the office day and night."

"Thanks, Dr…. Wait. Why is your last name not Morris?"

"Oh, it is, but I earned my degree and certification before Stanley asked me to marry him, so for professional purposes, I use my maiden name. Stanley is okay with that. He compromised since he dragged his feet when it came to proposing. We dated almost seven years before we got engaged."

"Seven. Wow. Why did you wait so long for a proposal?"

Would she wait that long for Brian to ask her hand in marriage? And why would that thought cross her mind so early in their relationship?

Pamela took a bite of cake and washed it down with a sip of coffee while she contemplated Melanie's question. She twisted her lips, rested her chin on her fist, and stared into the distance. "Well, honestly, we'd talked about it for quite a while, and we were both in school and then grad school. He focused on passing the certified public accountant exam, and I focused on becoming a licensed professional counselor. I guess we wanted to get that out of the way first, and so the day he found out he passed his exam, he proposed. We tied the knot six months later."

"Wow."

"See, Stanley is one of those men who wants to provide for his household financially, and he wanted to make sure he had himself together before he took on a wife. He's a Bible-reading man, so he fully believes a man needs to provide for his family spiritually and financially. I can appreciate that because he's done well by me. The long hours I still can't get with, but he's made sure I've never had to question his devotion to me."

Melanie took mental notes. Brian had become a lot like his dad—devoted and spiritual.

"Pam! You ladies need any help in there?" Stanley called to them.

"We're good. Be there in a sec." Pamela's voice carried into the family room, then she turned her attention back to Melanie with a softer tone, reached across the table and covered Melanie's hands with hers. "So, are we alright, dear?"

Melanie slowly released the air pent up in her chest and a this-is-too-good-to-be-true smile formed on her lips. Had they just shared a tender moment?

"Yes, ma'am. We're good."

"Okay. Let's get the guys' dessert to them, then I can show you baby pictures of Brian."

Melanie assisted Pamela with the preparation of dessert dishes and coffee for Brian and Stanley. Pamela and Melanie hummed along to the Christmas music that played in the family room. Something in the atmosphere shifted for Melanie and made her more comfortable after their conversation. She silently said a prayer of thanksgiving to God who allowed her to experience His love through the Morris family this Christmas.

They'd welcomed her into their home and shown kindness to her like they'd known her all her life, and for that, she couldn't be more grateful.

But the nagging sensation in the pit of her belly forced her to question if the warm, fuzzy feelings would soon come to an end.

Chapter 14

Brian leaned forward in his seat across from his dad, elbows rested on his knees, and watched Melanie follow Pamela into the kitchen. When they were out of view, he began, "So, Dad, what's up with Mom? I haven't seen her like this in years."

"What do you mean?" Stanley removed his glasses as if not having them on would allow him to hear and see more clearly.

"She's bubbly. Energetic, I guess. Just more into the holiday than usual. I'm not sure what it is. Can't quite put my finger on it." Brian stared in the direction of where she and Melanie exited the room.

"Well, for starters, you're home. It's not like we get to see much of you these days. I'm sure she's happy to have you here. She's always talking about you—you and your sister, for that matter."

"I didn't think it mattered."

"What?"

"Me coming around."

"And why would you say that?"

Brian raised his eyebrow with a you-know-what-I'm-talking-about look, but his dad's questioning expression remained the same.

"Just didn't feel like it mattered one way or the other if I was here."

There.

He'd said it.

And now that he managed to say it aloud and to someone else, it seemed silly. His own mother not wanting him around? That didn't come out the way he'd meant it by the change in his dad's eyes. They'd turned into slants, and whenever they did that, a lecture followed.

"You're the one who pulled away. She just allowed you to have the space you so desperately craved. At some point, I think she felt like she lost her connection to you and that you didn't need her anymore."

Brian's heart wept because of his father's apparent indifference regarding the situation and the pressing memories of when he made her feel like he didn't need her anymore. Did the high school stuff matter? At that time, he was learning himself and the world around him, trying to get a grip on who he was becoming. He'd told her many times he didn't need her advice, only to go to his father who he thought better suited to give him counsel.

But one of the most painful memories happened five years ago when he and Penelope's relationship ended. In Pamela's eyes, she was being motherly and helpful, but for Brian, she treated him like a patient. He'd stopped by her office to meet her for lunch, like they often did on Wednesday afternoons and shared the details of his breakup with Penelope after his mom prodded him about Penelope's whereabouts and happenings.

He gave Pamela the news, and she instantly gave unsolicited advice about his need to shift his priorities. He'd slammed his fist on the table, emphatically told her he didn't want or need her advice and to stay out of his personal life. He still recalled her blinking back tears before she reminded him he would never speak to her like that again. Though he apologized, their relationship hadn't been the same since that day.

Brian ran a hand over his cleanly shaven head. "Dad, it wasn't like that, and she knows it."

"Does she?" Stanley, a mirror image of what Brian would look like in thirty years, crinkled his eyebrows in the same fashion as Brian when he was confused.

"Look, it's not like I didn't apologize."

"Yeah, but you've been around long enough to know women are different. Your mother is different. You'd better be glad I wasn't with y'all that day." Stanley jabbed a finger in his direction, and Brian knew better than to comment after that and left the situation alone.

Stanley had always taught him to be honest and straightforward. Be a man of his word. Say what he meant and mean what he said. But suddenly he punished him for doing just that. How could he not have known that's why she acted differently toward him?

Could that have been the only situation that made her pull away? He racked his brain in recent years wondering what he did. Brian didn't want any emotional baggage to stand in the way of his relationship with Melanie. Whatever his and Pamela's issues were, he'd fix it.

∞

"Thanks for having me over." Melanie accepted hugs from both Pamela and Stanley. From dinner, opening presents, dessert, games, admiring baby pictures of Brian, and more dessert and family games, she was tired. Brian followed suit, helped Melanie into her coat, and grabbed to-go plates. At first Melanie declined, but Pamela insisted she take something with her so she wouldn't have to worry about making dinner for the next day or two.

"Merry Christmas. Hope to see you again sometime," Stanley said to Melanie. "Don't be a stranger, son." He pulled out of Brian's embrace.

"I won't, Dad. See you later," Brian called over his shoulder to them while he ushered Melanie to the car. Inside the warm and cozy house all day, the thought of warming the car for a few minutes escaped him before now.

"I should have let the car warm for a moment. I don't want you to freeze to death." Brian started the engine and turned the heat on full blast.

"Well, if we're freezing together, then it's all good."

Brian chuckled, blew into his hands, and rubbed them together. "I can think of a hundred things we can do together besides freeze."

"Oh, really?" Melanie shifted in her seat to face him, folded her bottom lip between her teeth, her eyes wide and playful. "Name one."

Brian's eyes trailed to her lips, but said, "Warm up in front of a fireplace and maybe watch a movie."

"I think I like that idea. You've got yourself another date."

Brian continued to rub his hands, the sound of which sounded like sandpaper. "I take it that means you enjoyed yourself today?"

"I did. Thank you for inviting me." Melanie covered the vents to warm her hands, but Brian took both of her hands in his and rubbed circles along the back of them with his thumbs.

"I know we haven't been seeing each other very long, and meeting my parents so soon was probably not on your to-do list, but I couldn't think of anywhere else for you to be other than with me."

He may as well have been drawing circles around her heart because the pulsing matched the pace of his hands. His eyes must have had a mind of their own because they pulled her in like a team winning a game of tug-of-war. Should she pull away? Though the inside of the car hadn't fully warmed, she started to melt.

Did he not know the effect he had on her?

"Are you ready to go home?"

Melanie cleared her throat, her eyebrows scrunched in confusion. *If I was ready before, I'm not ready anymore.* "What do you mean?"

"There's something I'd like to show you if you're not in a rush to get back. I know I've kept you out quite a bit today."

"No, no, you're fine. Show me." A you-know-I-want-to-spend-as-much-time-as-possible-with-you smile laced her lips.

Her heart had become a willing participant in whatever plans Brian had come up with. She'd go just about anywhere with him.

Brian kissed the back of her hands, released them, reduced the fan heat before he backed out of his parents' driveway. He drove about thirty minutes to the Ward Agricultural Center. During the drive, they discussed some of their treasured Christmas memories. He pulled up to the booth and handed the attendant his credit card to gain entrance to the Dancing Lights of Christmas show. Nearly every place of business closed on Christmas, and he had racked his brain and the internet looking for something to do with her just so they could spend a little more time together after leaving his parents' home. When he came across this show, he recalled how much she enjoyed the light tour they'd done a few weeks ago. This time it would only be the two of them along the two-and-a-half-mile route to see over two million lights dancing to Christmas music. For him, it was less about the event and more about spending time with her. It didn't matter what they did. For all he cared, they could have sat in the car and flicked a flashlight on and off if it meant he could be in her presence for a little while longer.

"Brian, this is beautiful. How did you find out about this?"

"Google."

Melanie covered his free hand with her own. "Thanks for making sure I didn't spend today by myself. I appreciate that."

"Anything to put a smile on your face. That reminds me: I have something for you." He glanced in the rearview mirror and checked to see if any cars were behind him before he stopped and reached into the backseat. He pulled out a small green-and-red gift bag and handed it to her.

"I thought we agreed not to trade gifts."

"You agreed; I didn't."

Melanie recalled the conversation and snickered. He was indeed right. Less pressure on him to search for the perfect present. Besides, there wasn't anything she wanted. Brian handed the gift bag to her and resumed driving along the route. Her heart sped up a minute when she removed the small jewelry box from the bag, but it was way too early in their relationship for him to propose, so the thought vanished and her heartbeat slowed to normal. She opened the box and found a pair of angel-shaped earrings trimmed in diamonds.

"These are beautiful, Brian." She leaned over the center console, kissed his cheek softly, and lingered for a moment longer than she intended, his woodsy, masculine cologne made him more attractive, though he didn't need any assistance. The closeness surged feelings within her she suppressed because she'd only been dating him a month. "Thank you."

She returned to her seat with her eyes bulged at the feelings she'd experienced and hoped the glow from the dancing lights didn't give her face away.

"You're welcome. I saw them, and they reminded me of you. An angel." Brian linked his hand in hers and brought it to his lips but didn't release it afterward. "So beautiful," Brian commented.

"Yeah, very much so."

Neither was speaking of the lights but the moment they shared. Weren't there rules against having feelings for someone you hadn't known very long? Maybe she needed to take a step back to make sure it wasn't all in her head? Did she and Brian truly have a connection and were her feelings real? Perhaps that was something that should be explored with her therapist—a new one, someone who was not Brian's mother.

Chapter 15

Melanie threw herself on the bed. That kiss on her doorstep confirmed it. She'd fallen hard for Brian.

Ridiculously hard.

Like a giddy-lovesick-teenager-kind-of-hard, and for what?

Part of her wanted to be free and allow this thing between them to develop naturally, but shouldn't there be some type of rules about falling too quickly? She'd once heard someone say you needed to know a person in all four seasons before deciding whether you wanted to be with them. Was she overthinking it? It wasn't like he'd proposed to her and she'd said yes. She'd only spent the evening with him.

An evening that solidified her feelings for him.

"When I'm not with him, I'm thinking about him. Maybe I'm thinking about him too much. Is there even such a thing as too much? Am I moving too fast or thinking about this all wrong? Ugh, I'm starting to sound crazy, even to me."

She rolled over and grabbed her journal and pen off the nightstand. When she wrote her thoughts down, it didn't feel as crazy as saying them out loud. Though journaling refreshed her, she preferred to talk things out with someone. Usually in situations like this, she'd talk to Natalie or Charise. She chuckled to herself because their advice would always be drastically different.

Natalie, being the free spirit she was, would tell her to go for it, not worrying about how things would turn out. Just live and enjoy the moment. She paused to consider how she'd made progress because of her therapy sessions. The thought of Natalie didn't bring about tears as they had the past few months.

Charise, being the more sensible friend, would tell her to take her time and enjoy getting to know Brian. Charise married right out of college, and her advice to anyone who'd listen would be to take things slowly, something she wished she had done. Charise wanted every letter surrounding her name she could get. She had three goals in college: get married, earn her degree, and join her sorority. Thirty had been her magic number, and she had to have her husband and children before then.

Melanie thought of Charise and Natalie, hoping to find a happy medium in between. They were both usually right, but the key word was *balance,* something she often lacked. Melanie needed to know which way she was going and forge a plan to get there. She didn't like not knowing, but at this point in their relationship, she couldn't really expect Brian to know either.

Lately, her go-to person had been her therapist, but that was Brian's mother. How could she share her deepest thoughts and feelings about her life or her life with Brian with his mother? Her phone rang and jolted her from her thoughts.

Melanie slid her thumb across the screen to answer Brian's call. "Hey. Made it home already?"

"Not quite. Are you alright?"

"I am. Is everything okay?" Melanie sensed the hesitation in his voice, which put her on high alert.

"Yeah. I've got you on my mind. Can I pick you up tomorrow so we can talk?"

"That sounds good, but are you sure everything is okay?" Melanie rose to a sitting position, her temple pulsing at the idea something could be wrong between them. Didn't they just spend Christmas together?

"Yeah, yeah, no worries," Brian said confidently. "I just want to spend time with you before things get crazy at work again."

"Well, then it's a date." Her heart rate returned to a steady rhythm with Brian's reassurance. "What time do I need to be ready?"

"Six o'clock."

"Okay, see you at six."

"I'll let you get your rest, and I'll see your beautiful face tomorrow. Night." His baritone voice enveloped her like a down comforter on a cool winter night. A voice she wouldn't mind hearing every evening because it brought about a coziness and contentment to her soul.

"Night."

Melanie flung herself back across the bed and prayed, "Lord, only You know how this whole thing will turn out, so please, please, please, help me not to worry or rush. I want to do this—whatever *this* is—in your timing. In Jesus' name. Amen."

Chapter 16

Melanie danced in the mirror while she dressed for her date with Brian. The thought of him brought about a sense of giddiness she'd never experienced in any other relationship. Tomorrow she'd be back at work styling and pampering her clients, but today was about her and Brian, and excitement bubbled within her at the thought of being with him again.

A surprise outing.

Brian refused to tell her his plans for them. She loved surprises— romantic surprises— though that didn't stop her from wracking her brain to figure out what they could do a couple of days after Christmas.

A quick glance at the clock told her she'd enjoyed herself too much during her solo dance marathon because she only had about ten minutes left to get ready before Brian was scheduled to arrive. Her phone rung. Had he arrived early?

Typical Brian.

"Hey!"

"You sound refreshed."

His voice did more for her energy level than a morning cup of coffee. "I feel pretty good. You pulling up?"

"I'll be there in five. Do you need more time to get ready? I could make a pit stop and grab coffee for us."

"No. I'm good. Are we going to be outside?" Melanie mentally ran through a few outside date scenarios since Brian had been adamant about keeping their date location a surprise.

"Maybe. Maybe not. You don't have to wait much longer. Hang in there. Just know that you'll love it."

"Okay. I give up. I'll be ready when you get here. Drive safely."

"I will. See you soon," Brian said before he ended the call.

Brian's call made her rethink her ensemble. For him to ask about coffee in the evening made her think she needed to keep warm. Surely, this would be some sort of an outside date and that spelled sweater and jeans and not the sweater dress she planned to wear, even if paired with riding boots. As promised, Brian rang her doorbell five minutes later, his knit cap pulled down enough to cover his ears. His hands rested in his jacket pockets until he locked eyes with her.

"Hey, Mel. It's good to see your face. Come here." Brian flashed a smile that made her insides melt and drew her closer to him.

Just about everyone she knew shortened her name and called her Mel, but no one said it quite like Brian. A thirst only his voice could fill. Every time her name poured from his lips, her heart pitter-pattered a little faster and a knot formed and released in the pit of her belly.

"Consider my face your belated Christmas present."

Brian chuckled. "Still with the jokes I see, but since you put it that way, it's my favorite gift."

She stepped closer and encircled her arms around his neck. He smelled good. Whatever his cologne, it lingered on her clothes last night and would do the same today. A scent she committed to memory. "You can step in out of the cold for a second. Let me grab my things and turn off the lights."

Brian stepped in but kept the door open.

"Hey, I'm ready." Melanie returned fully dressed in her riding boots and pea coat, purse hanging on her arm.

Brian walked out of the door, stood behind her while she locked up, took her hand in his and led her to the passenger-side door. He didn't move to join her in the car until she secured her seatbelt.

"Nice and warm in here." Melanie clapped her hands. "So where are we going?"

"The suspense is killing you, isn't it?" The corners of his lips turned up into an I-know-something-you-don't-know smile.

She pinched her thumb and forefinger together. "A little."

"How about you try to guess, and I'll let you know if you're hot or cold?"

"Okay. Is it outside?"

"You're warm. Keep trying."

"Wait. Is this pea coat enough to keep me warm? Do we need to turn around so I can grab a heavier coat?"

"I don't think so. I can keep you warm if you get cold, so no need to worry about that."

Melanie's eyes trailed to the expanse of his broad chest, and she chewed her bottom lip. She tugged at the collar of her sweater to fan the spiral of warmth that shot through her body. "Okay."

Now would be an appropriate time for a bottle of water or anything to moisturize her drying mouth.

"Giving up already?"

"No, no. Thinking, that's all. Can't be the tour of lights because we've done that already. I guess I have no idea."

"You're actually quite close. We're going to the Gaylord Opryland Resort."

Brian mentioned the resort like she frequented often. Why would she be excited about that?

"I don't get it. What's going on there?" Could he sense her disappointment? That was not her idea of a surprise.

"That's the surprise."

"You're lucky you're handsome."

"If that wins me points with you, then I guess I am." Brian lifted her hand and brushed it with a soft kiss that set off a rippled tingling effect from her hand to her toes. A quick uncontrollable shiver followed.

This man would be her undoing.

Brian parked in the Opry Mills mall parking lot, and they walked the remainder of the way to the resort with Melanie's hand tucked securely in his.

Wow escaped Melanie's lips the moment they stepped through the entrance.

"This is amazing, Brian. You've been paying attention. You know how much I love the Christmas season. This is pure magic."

"I knew you'd like it, but this isn't the surprise." Brian's chest swelled proudly with gratitude. Anything he could do to be the reason behind the smile on her face was worth it.

Melanie's mouth formed and O and her eyes twinkled as much as the lights before them. "I can't wait to see what tops this."

Over three million lights hung throughout the resort and transformed it into a magical wonderland. Were they in Nashville or on a romantic getaway? Christmas tunes, palm trees, and poinsettias added to the festive atmosphere.

Brian and Melanie walked as much of the resort as they could amid the crowd. After excusing themselves at least five times, Brian bent toward her ear. "This is nice, but more crowded than I thought it would be. Let's head out for your treat."

Melanie tilted her head and grinned in response. If she had issues with navigating through the crowd, he couldn't see it in her face. Her smile, as bright as the millions of lights twinkling throughout the building, nourished his soul.

Brian led her to Magnolia lobby and checked his watch. Perfect timing. Ten more minutes. He squeezed her hand. "Ready?"

"As much as I'll ever be."

When Brian led her outside, Melanie stopped short when the gust of wind nearly knocked them back inside. Melanie's hands flew to her mouth. She squealed when the white horse and carriage approached.

"Really, Brian?" Melanie bit down on her bottom lip and her eyebrows stretched higher than he'd ever seen them.

He handed his phone to the attendant to scan their tickets. "Yes, for you." Brian grinned and squeezed her hand a little tighter.

Once inside the carriage—a bit uncomfortable for him with the canopy an inch above his head—Brian studied her. He'd take the twelve-minute ride a thousand times to witness the gleam in her eyes.

"You think of everything, don't you?"

"No. Only you. How'd I do?"

A slight jolt of the carriage and the clicking of the horse's hooves signaled the start of the tour around the Gaylord Opryland Resort.

Melanie waved her hand. "Look at these lights and decorations. You did good. Thank you, Brian." Her eyes and smile were in sync. A forever kind of smile. One that spoke to his soul.

"Anything for you, which reminds me of what I want to talk with you about. Please stop me if I start sounding crazy."

"Okay. Pinkie swear." Melanie shifted in her seat.

"This last month or so has been surreal. I enjoy spending time with you, and I don't want this to end. I feel like we've connected on so many levels: spiritually, mentally, and emotionally. Do you feel the same?" He caressed the back of her hand and waited for her to answer.

"I do." Melanie stroked his cheek with her index finger and smiled. A smile that encouraged him to communicate his emotions.

Foreign communication.

It'd been years since he'd talked about his feelings with a woman, and even so, he'd never felt this way about any other woman, not even Penelope, perhaps that's why it had been so easy to choose his career over their relationship. He was sure to make mistakes with Melanie, but that wouldn't be one of them.

He'd choose her every single time.

"I'm not asking you to marry me yet, but I would like us to be committed to each other, to see where this goes. You're the only woman I want to see, the only woman in my life, and I'd like to be the only man in yours."

She stroked his cheek again. "You are, Brian."

"Mel, I want it to be you and me. It may seem sudden for you, but it isn't for me. I wanted to ask you out the moment I laid eyes on you the evening of the incident, but that was neither the place nor the time. I thought I'd lost my chance forever—until I walked into your salon with the toy drive flyer. I don't think me seeing you again was by accident, and I don't want to miss the opportunity to tell you how I feel."

"You have no idea how glad I am to hear you say that. I want the same thing. Us. I enjoy getting to know you and who I am when I'm with you," she finally said.

"Then it's settled. You and me."

Brian didn't wait for another word. He intertwined his fingers in her tight curls behind her head and drew her closer to his lips. If he had any doubt about his feelings for her or vice versa, they vanished the moment their lips met. More immaculate than the lights throughout the resort grounds, their connection had been solidified.

Desire coursed through him.

Desire for Melanie to be a part of his soul.

Desire for her to be his forever.

Chapter 17

Melanie's relationship with Brian was nothing short of the pages from one of her favorite romance novels. She never had to guess what he thought or if he was thinking of her because he made sure to call or text to check in with her day-to-day to see if she needed anything. He brought lunch, coffee, or even dinner to her when she had busy days in the salon.

Melanie joined him for New Year's Eve service at his church, and he visited her church the following Sunday. Attending service together had become a regular thing for them, though she mostly visited his church since he served in ministry. She, on the other hand, had been content with paying her tithes and sitting in the pews. But Brian's passion for serving stirred something within her, made her rethink her role in servitude.

Melanie finished up her last client so she could make her appointment with Dr. Williams. She hadn't had any communication with her since Christmas Day, and so much had transpired since the last time she saw her as her therapist.

Melanie twisted her client Danielle around to face the mirror, added finishing spray, and fixed a curl here and there before Danielle's final approval. She received payment, confirmed Danielle's next appointment, hugged her, and saw her out the door. Melanie swept up loose hair clippings, wiped down the seats and shampoo bowl, turned off her radio, grabbed her things, and locked up the shop to leave for her therapist appointment.

On the drive, she rehearsed what she would say to Dr. Williams, but nothing seemed to come out right. How would her relationship with Brian affect their doctor/patient relationship until she could find a new therapist? Dr. Williams had been brief in their conversation on Christmas Day regarding their discussions remaining private, but surely it couldn't all be that easy.

Melanie pulled into a parking space near the entrance and checked her hair and makeup. Why was she stalling? Her hair and makeup were fine when she left work twenty minutes ago. The anxiety she had when she learned Dr. Williams was Brian's mother resurfaced. Something told her she shouldn't worry though. Dr. Williams was the professional, and she would know how to handle this situation.

Follow her lead.

She shut the engine, pulled her coat back on, and raced to the entrance, dodging the wind. Her feet shuffled faster than her mind wanted her to go. As much as she needed to talk to Dr. Williams, she couldn't shake the eerie feeling about this visit.

As had been her routine for the past several months, she walked into the modest office lobby that only housed a small table and two purple cushioned office chairs and flipped the switch that notified Dr. Williams she had arrived. She grabbed a magazine, took a seat in one of the cushioned chairs, and thumbed through it with shaky hands, not really reading any of the pages, only forcing herself to keep busy while she waited. She wriggled her nose. Had the lobby always smelled like a combination of Febreze and staleness?

"Melanie, good afternoon. Come on back," Dr. Williams greeted her, holding the privacy door open for her to gain entry. "How've you been?"

"Great, actually. You?" Melanie answered with a plastered smile. Good thing Dr. Williams showed up when she did. Melanie had started to notice all the imperfections in the lobby, which were quite the opposite of Dr. Williams' private office.

"Come right on in and have a seat on the couch."

Melanie sat this time, as opposed to lying down. Her scalp tingled, and her throat suddenly parched. Dr. Williams hadn't kept the pleasantries going as she normally would have.

Was something wrong?

What happened to her?

Was she no longer keeping her work and personal life separate like she professed to doing when Melanie spent time with her and her family on Christmas Day? She watched Dr. Williams sign and shuffle a few papers around before she put them in a catalogue envelope, fastened it, and handed them to her.

"Here you go. These are for you. Per the code of ethics, we are not to have a dual relationship. We are only to know one another in a professional manner. Your relationship with Brian changes that. This is our last visit, Melanie. I've referred you to Dr. Wang, who is located on the third floor of this building. Of course, you may see her or find another therapist of your choice."

Dr. Williams' tone and posture remained professional, yet stoic. Where was the woman she talked with over coffee and German chocolate cake?

"Wait, what?" Melanie's eyelids fluttered and she swallowed what felt like grains of sand. Her trembling hands searched for something to hold on to. She gripped the sofa arm. It seemed someone pulled a rug from under her, yet she wasn't standing. "I thought you said everything was okay and that we didn't have to share anything with Brian." Though terminating their patient-therapist relationship was the best choice, Melanie had hoped to do it on her own terms, but Pamela snatched the bandage off with no mercy.

"You're absolutely correct, but now that I know it's you he's seeing, I can no longer be your therapist."

"I just assumed we could continue," Melanie said, though that wasn't entirely true. She was so taken aback by the news, she forgot she'd already decided to end her sessions with Dr. Williams because of her relationship with Brian. It would have been too weird anyway, given the fact she was the mother to the man she cared so much about.

"I'm sorry, but rules are rules. The board is serious when it comes to dual relationships. I hope I've been able to help you, and I'm sorry we can't continue." Dr. Williams pressed her lips in a taut line.

"Well, okay then." Melanie took a deep breath and stood to leave. This had to be the reason why she felt so awkward on the drive over. Her instincts had been on point in warning her things were about to go sideways. Melanie extended her hand for a farewell handshake.

"But," Dr. Williams accepted Melanie's hand and held it firmly, "we could continue your therapy if you stop seeing Brian."

Melanie's eyes filled with tears, and she yanked her hand away like she'd touched an open flame.

"What? What did you say?"

Dr. Williams held her hands up in surrender, folded her lips, and shook her head, her eyes void of any emotion. Melanie couldn't read her.

Where was the woman who warmly greeted her on Christmas Day? Purchased small trinkets for her?

Played board games and shared a meal with her?

Hugged her warmly and treated her like she was part of their family?

Was that just an act? Surely Dr. Williams had to be playing with her emotions.

"I'm sorry, Melanie. Those are your choices. Your relationship with Brian or your therapeutic relationship with me."

The progress she'd made because of Dr. Williams' assistance caused her to briefly consider her options. Dr. Williams helped her uncover and cope with the pain she'd tucked away long before the loss of her friend, Natalie. In a sense, she'd used Dr. Williams as a substitute to replace the relationship she had with her deceased mother. Part of her felt like she needed their relationship. Sure, she could easily see another therapist, but would she receive the same level of care?

The promises she and Brian had recently made to each other flooded her mind at Dr. Williams' words. Melanie wiped at the tears that wouldn't stay at bay. She breathed heavier with each passing moment. She couldn't care less about dual relationships, or anything else. She'd finally met the man she wanted to spend most of her days with, and the thought of not doing so—of the possibility of that being ripped away so suddenly because of her seeing a therapist, this therapist, his mother—constricted her breathing and tightened her airwaves.

Ending her relationship with him was not an option.

Chapter 18

The moment she saw Dr. Williams' face on Christmas Day, Melanie knew this situation would get complicated. She sat in her car, unable to bring herself to shift it into gear. Why did her terminated patient-therapist relationship feel like she'd lost her mother all over again? How had it come to this? Or to not see Brian? No way she could break it off with him because of her misplaced emotional ties to his mother.

The thought of that sounded crazy, even to her.

She rested her head against the headrest and closed her eyes, took several deep breaths, wiped her tears, and shifted the car into reverse. Her phone vibrated, and Brian's number and picture appeared on the screen.

Her heart sank.

Had this been forty-five minutes ago, she would have answered quickly, but now her thoughts were all over the place. She silenced the vibration without declining the call so he wouldn't get the impression she'd ignored him.

She just needed some time to clear her head.

Her mind still in a fog, she drove around town with no real destination in mind. Who could she use as a sounding board? If this were any other situation, she would go directly to Brian, but she couldn't take this to him until she felt better about it. Charise would be home with her kids, and she hated to bother her, but she was the only choice—the only other person she trusted to share parts of her personal life with aside from Brian and her ex-therapist.

Melanie tapped the voice recognition button on her steering wheel and gave the voice command to call Charise. When Charise said her company would be welcomed, she hung up and followed the course to her house from memory. Though it had been quite a while since she last visited, Charise's fancy neighborhood was hard to forget.

When Melanie pulled up to the entry gate of Alpine Trove, the guard asked for her ID and the address she intended to visit. He copied her information onto his notepad, spoke into his walkie-talkie attached to his coat, and pushed a button to open the gate that allowed her entry.

The landscaping was well kept, even for the winter season. Purple flowers and greenery lined the streets the same as it did in spring. Melanie took a right at the first stop sign, right past the water fountain with Alpine Trove in lights. Charise's two-story brick house was in the cul-de-sac at her next left turn. Melanie pulled into the driveway at the signal of Charise who stood in the doorway dressed in a vanilla sweater and black leggings.

"So good to see you outside of the shop. What's going on, girl?" Charise gave her a quick hug at the door and stepped aside to let her in.

Apple cinnamon. The scent reminded her of Christmas and now, Brian, who she associated with Christmas because of the sweet memories they created. Melanie followed Charise through the hallway and arched entryway into the kitchen, noting the family portraits and abstract paintings along the walls.

"You guys painted?"

"Yeah. Jeff and I thought to hide the shenanigans of these children. I don't even think I told you that Jeff Jr. decided to display his writing skills on my wall. I'm glad he's learning in kindergarten, but to print his name on the wall to prove it is not cool. I mean, who does that and writes their own name?"

Melanie chuckled. "I'm sure every five-year-old has done it once or twice."

"Seriously. I think if I were to do it, I'd leave my name out of it, or heck, put my sister's name on the wall. Well, come to think of it, he wrote, 'Jeff, Mom, and Jess.'"

Melanie chuckled louder.

"I'm glad you're tickled."

"Speaking of them, where are the kids?" Melanie shrugged out of her coat and handed it and her purse to Charise to put away, then she sat at the counter height bar.

"When the baby went down, I managed to get Jeff and Jess to nap as well. Your timing is perfect. Coffee?" Charise hung Melanie's coat and purse in the coat closet then maneuvered around the chef's kitchen to grab K-cups for the Keurig.

"You drink coffee at four in the afternoon? I'd think you'd be trying to wind down, not up."

"Never know what's going to go on around these parts. School is still out, remember? They go back next week. Besides, I don't really drink it for the caffeine—I like the flavor. I also have tea and hot chocolate. What suits you?" Charise pulled out the drawer for Melanie to choose.

"I suppose I can have a coffee, too. What kind of creamer do you have?"

"Name it, and I probably have it."

"*Hmmm.* Caramel Macchiato?"

"Coming right up."

Charise brewed both of their cups before she dived into the reason for Melanie's visit. Charise invited her into the living room where they sat opposite each other in matching recliners in front of the fireplace.

Charise folded a leg underneath her, shifted her weight onto one elbow, and leaned in, poised to hear whatever Melanie had to say. "So…what's going on?"

Melanie took a sip of her coffee before she answered. "A lot and nothing."

"I want to talk about the 'a lot.' Clearly it's bothering you enough to drive all the way out here."

"What? I've come out here before."

"But it's been about a year since your last visit. I don't have to tell you these children are unpredictable, and our alone time is limited. If you have something to say, you need to say it now."

Charise had a point. Melanie wasn't accustomed to being around small children, but from many of the conversations they'd had at her shop, they required a lot of attention.

"You know I started seeing a therapist after Natalie, right?"

"Ummm-hmmm," Charise mumbled, nodded over her coffee mug, encouraging her to continue.

"Turns out she's Brian's mother, and I don't know what to do about it, but she does. I can't see her anymore because of some dual relationship, or she says I could stop seeing him. In some way, I feel like I still need her, too. She reminds me of my mom."

"Wow." Charise's eyes bulged at the revelation. "I'm sorry, Mel. The fact you admitted she reminds you of your mom probably means you need to see someone else anyway. I know you miss your mom, honey, but you can't replace her." Charise gave Melanie's hand a reassuring squeeze. "Have you talked to Brian about it?"

"No, not yet. Shoot. I don't even know what to say. I mean, I can't just break it off with him because of some stupid dual relationship stuff she brought up. If you ask me, my relationship with him shouldn't have anything to do with her. He isn't my therapist. She is. And sadly, I sort of feel like I need her."

Charise cupped Melanie's hand. "Sweetie, you do know there are other therapists around here, right?"

"Yeah, but I don't know. I don't like the idea of opening up to everybody. Kinda felt like she was it. I really like her."

"Well, who do you like more?" Charise's eyebrows hiked up.

"We both know the answer to that."

"Hmmm." Charise sipped her coffee and gazed into the flames dancing in the fireplace. "I'm sorry, Mel, but it's rare to find someone you care about and you can connect with on many levels. I think as we get older, it gets harder. Hmph, I think you already know what my advice is."

Melanie squeezed her shoulders and flashed an I-know-what-you're-thinking-smile. "Yeah, I do."

"Good, and can I just say I knew it," Charise snapped her fingers. "the moment he stepped into your shop. I should be a matchmaker."

"I don't know why. You didn't do any matching."

"Well, almost."

They shared a laugh. Charise couldn't tell her exactly what to do, but talking with her helped Melanie's anxiety a little.

Melanie sipped her coffee. This was cozy. She would much rather sit around the fireplace and chat with Brian about anything rather than sit here with Charise, not that she didn't enjoy the girl time. The thought of losing him brought about the strong realization that her feelings for Brian were deeper than she fathomed.

How could she make any other choice?

Chapter 19

Brian stood on the other side of the privacy glass while his partner questioned the bartender about Brittany's death in the interrogation room. They'd picked him up at the bar that evening after they received and reviewed video footage of his argument and tussle with Brittany from her alarm company. The company had been slow in providing the information, citing privacy issues, until they received a warrant.

Mark slouched in the stainless-steel chair bolted to the floor with his arms folded across his chest.

"I'm not saying anything until I get a lawyer," he said repeatedly.

Brian remained on the opposite side of the two-way mirror and allowed Detective Farrington to take the lead on the investigation — gave him a chance to show off his skills as Brian listened and assessed the information—or lack thereof—that he got out of Mark. Detective Farrington abruptly stood and walked around to sit on the edge of the table and used his closeness to intimidate Mark. He slammed the file down on the table and opened it to show Mark the camera shots of him and Brittany.

"Since you won't talk, I guess I'll just tell you what I think happened. Brittany, your neighbor, was a beautiful woman who frequented your bar with her girlfriends. You became fond of her, gave her free drinks from time to time until she eventually decided to go out on a date with you. You went out several times and even spent evenings in her place. Your feelings grew and hers didn't—at least not in the way you would have liked. She wanted to break things off when she saw you were getting too serious, and you couldn't handle it. So, what do you do? Kill her. If you couldn't have her, nobody would. You thought you got away with it because it was dark, usually quiet and exclusive neighborhood so no one was around, except you didn't count on the camera footage or us finding out that the security cameras had been tampered with after the fact. Sure, you wiped your prints, but you didn't know her security company backs up security footage when the cameras go offline. Look at this." Detective Farrington tapped the timestamp on the photo. "You see, that's you coming out of her house approximately fifteen minutes after you killed her." He flipped to the next photo. "And that's also you running across the lawn to your house."

"And you said you were…taking a nap when you heard tires screeching," Detective Farrington flipped through his notepad. "Did I miss anything?"

"Just stop," Mark screamed, repeatedly raked his hands through his hair, and sobbed.

"Well, I'll be…" Brian's spine straightened, and ears perked up on the opposite side of the two-way mirror. The interrogation didn't even last a full hour. *"Hmph."*

He checked his phone for messages, though it didn't ring or vibrate, and hoped to see something from Melanie. It wasn't like her to not return his call or text. It had been a day since he'd last heard from her, and he became concerned. He silently prayed she was okay. It took everything in him not to stop by her shop on his way in that morning.

He slid the phone back into his belt clip and listened intently to Mark's confession.

"I didn't mean to kill her. We were having a good time, eating dinner, and sharing a bottle of wine. She invited me over—said she wanted to talk about us. Yeah, I liked her. Good people. I felt light when she was around. Beautiful smile and spirit. Funny, too," Mark reflected.

Detective Farrington nodded toward the two-way mirror at Brian, returned to his seat and listened to Mark's confession.

"She told me she liked hanging out with me, but we had to stop. She hooked back up with her old boyfriend, something about him coming to live with her and we could no longer see each other. He's jealous, protective, and she'd rather I act like I didn't know her. She said that would be our last interaction. She wouldn't come to my bar anymore and I couldn't just drop by her house. It would be as if we'd never known each other. We'd been seeing each other six months, so I couldn't believe she could walk away just like that." Mark paused and rubbed his temples. The memory haunting and taunting him.

"We argued, and it escalated into a fight. I–I–I've never even hit a woman before, so I don't know where the rage came from. I didn't mean to hurt her. I never wanted to hurt her. I just wanted her to see she was making a big mistake. It got complicated fast. I don't know what came over me and what would even possess me to reach for my gun. I'm so sorry."

"Me, too." Detective Farrington stood, secured Mark's hands behind his back, and read him his rights. "Mark Delcaro, you are under arrest for the murder of Brittany Gibson. You have the right to remain silent. Anything you say can and will be used against you in a court of law. You have the right to an attorney. If you can't afford one, one will be provided to you."

When Detective Farrington escorted Mark out of the interrogation room, Brian stopped the recording. He stared into the now empty room and reflected on the case. Though he was confident Mark was their guy and he'd confessed, something still didn't feel quite right. Too easy. Detective Farrington walked into the room and interrupted his thoughts.

"What does your instinct tell you?" Brian asked.

"What do you mean? About what?" Frown lines appeared on Detective Farrington's forehead and his eyebrows moved closer together.

"This."

"We got our guy. My first murder case solved. A win to me. Come on. Let's go deliver the news to Brittany's relatives," Detective Farrington declared triumphantly, chest puffed, hands tucked in his pockets. Proud, Brian could see that.

"You got it. I'll stick around here and handle the rest of the paperwork." Brian grabbed his notes and coffee and headed back to his desk. He couldn't shake the feeling that something was off. Was it because he hadn't heard from Melanie?

Nothing could possibly be wrong between the two of them.

Could it?

Didn't they just declare their feelings and make a commitment to each other? Or maybe something really was off with the case?

Something.

Either way, he wouldn't rest until he found the source of the unnerving feeling.

Chapter 20

Another missed call from Brian.

Melanie responded to some of his texts over the last week but kept her replies brief. Her decision to continue seeing him was not supposed to be dry and almost nonexistent as it had been. She'd been busy and could have made time for him if she wanted to, but uncertainty brewed within her about how to have that conversation with him—the conversation where she'd share she'd known his mom for months as her therapist and the only way to continue her therapy with her was to end her relationship with him.

Didn't she need them both?

She sighed, swept hair into the dustpan, and listened to contemporary gospel tunes on her radio. All the messages were the same: everything would work out, give it to Jesus, depend on the Lord. She wasn't even sure how it would work out or how to give this to Jesus. She had been sure of herself when she sat with Charise, but every time she saw Brian's number on her phone screen, she clammed up.

But the weekend was coming.

She'd given herself until then to talk with him so he wouldn't get the idea she'd backed out of her commitment to date him exclusively. That was the last thing she wanted. In fact, she craved his presence more than her morning coffee – and she had to have it every day.

Since Melanie's last visit with Dr. Williams, it became clearer she wanted far more with Brian than she currently had. The thought of losing him was too much to stomach.

It took her ten minutes to sweep the floor, a task that should only take two minutes, three tops, given the small space, but she couldn't help mulling over what to do next. She had slipped behind the curtain to put away the broom and dustpan when she heard a knock on the door. Instead of calling out to allow entry, she walked over and opened it.

Brian.

She should have known he would show up eventually.

"Hey, Mel. Is everything okay? I've been calling you like crazy. I was starting to worry." Brian immediately pulled her into his arms and held her like it had been years since they last saw each other.

"Hey, Brian." Melanie wrapped her arms around his waist and rested her head on his broad chest. The erratic pulsing of his heartbeat matched hers. "I'm okay. How are you?"

"Not okay." He stepped out of her embrace into the salon and closed the door behind him. "Did I do something wrong? You've been avoiding me." The worry lines etched across his forehead and the hurt in his eyes sank her heart like the Titanic.

Melanie averted her eyes, doing everything in her power to avoid eye contact. She went to the closet and rearranged bottles of shampoos and conditioners. "No, you haven't done anything, Brian." Should she say something else to give him more assurance? Probably, but words escaped her. At least she had nothing to say that wouldn't point blame.

He gently tugged her hand and pulled her away from the cabinet and onto the small sofa next to him.

"Please talk to me, Mel. I haven't been able to concentrate at work. You're all I've been thinking about, and I've been wracking my brain going over our last conversations, trying to figure out if it was something I said or if I'm moving too fast for you. If that's the case, we can slow down. I just don't want to lose you. What is it? How can I make this right?"

His eyes pleaded with her just as much as his words, and her heart shattered into pieces. His beautiful light brown orbs always did something to her heartstrings.

No way she could withhold the truth with such a heartfelt request. She took a deep breath and started from the beginning.

"I had trouble forgiving myself for going against the inkling in my spirit that warned me not to go out with Natalie the day she died. I knew we should have stayed at my house or found something else to do, but we went anyway, and now Natalie's gone." Melanie stopped and took a deep breath to push back the sorrow that rose within her.

Why was she telling this story in the first place?

"So, I went to see a therapist who helped me through my grief, my guilt, and other issues I've allowed to hold me back. She was wonderful. Turns out, the therapist is your mother."

"Oh, no." Brian interrupted her and squeezed her hands gently. "Is that what this is about? You think she's going to share confidential information with me? Melanie, you don't have to—"

"No, no, that's not it. Let me finish," she interjected. "I'm not seeing her anymore as of about a week ago. Something about dual relationships. She can only know me as a client and nothing more."

"Because of me. I'm sorry."

"Right. But she gave me a choice. If I wanted to continue seeing her, I had to end my relationship with you. And not having you in my life isn't an option, but I feel a little lost without continuing therapy with her. Maybe I've started using her as a crutch, I don't know, but I'll figure it out. I'm sorry. I didn't know how to share that with you."

"Wow. I'm so sorry, Mel. What do you want to do?" Brian slid closer to her, slipped an arm around her shoulder, and squeezed.

"I want you."

"And this is why you've been avoiding me." His voice was low. He rested his head against hers in deep thought.

"Not quite avoiding you but trying to figure out how to move forward. Brian—" She shifted in her seat, folded one leg under her bottom, and turned his face toward hers with one finger— "I don't plan to stop seeing you. I never did. I enjoy you and every moment we spend together. I don't even know how to explain my happiness with our relationship."

Brian stroked her chin, and his eyes professed his love for her. "I have to say I'm relieved. I thought you'd changed your mind about wanting to be committed to me. I was so sure we were on the same page and then to not hear from you caused me to worry. I don't want to lose you, Mel, especially over something like this."

Melanie covered his hands with hers. "It's hard for me to put into words, Brian. When I found out she was your mother, I knew I wouldn't be able to continue seeing her as my therapist long term, but I thought I'd be able to end my therapy with her on my own terms."

"I get it, I think. I'll talk to my mom about this, okay?"

"Should we talk to her together?" Melanie surprised herself by asking to go along with him.

"I'd like to talk to her first. There are some other things we need to discuss, but this has moved to the top of my list. Surely, there's a way where our being together shouldn't affect her being your therapist, at least for a little while longer. That is what you want, isn't it?"

"Yeah. I love you so much." Melanie threw herself into his arms.

"I love you, too, and only God can stand in the way of us being together." Brian kissed the top of her head and squeezed tighter.

Melanie had just professed her love for him. She'd hoped it would happen over a romantic dinner or something, not while they sat in her salon figuring out how to move forward in their relationship. Would he think she was simply caught up in the moment and overcome with emotion?

For her, it was real.

Was it real for him, too?

Chapter 21

Brian stormed into Pamela's office uninvited and demanded she speak with him.

"Why do you always have to be so extreme? I can't believe you told Melanie to choose between me and you." Brian huffed with fire in his eyes, his eyebrows furrowed. He loved his mother, and he wouldn't dare disrespect her again and yell, but he'd hope she could understand how upset he was.

Pamela sat back in her leather seat behind the desk, shoulders relaxed, with her fingers laced across her belly. She looked him square in the eyes, her tone even. "I have to take precaution, Brian, and you know that. I can't get into trouble with the board again. I'll never again jeopardize my career for anyone, no matter who it is."

"This is not the same situation—completely different—and you know it."

Pamela shrugged and shuffled papers around her desk as if to dismiss him. "I'm not in the mood to have this discussion, Brian."

Brian paced back and forth. "And why not? You know how important Melanie is to me and how important this therapy is to her. Why would you ask her to choose? You've been helping her all this time. Why do you have to stop now?"

Without looking at him, she asked, "Don't you remember Trevor?"

"Yeah, I remember. His wife thought you had a thing going on with him because you hugged him in church. I get that, but you know that sort of thing isn't going to happen with Melanie."

"The circumstances are different, but it's best to end her therapy now, before things get too serious between the two of you. Even the fact that she's seeing you now creates blurred lines. Our relationship can be viewed by the board as a dual relationship. None of it is worth it. Can you even imagine how I felt when I received a letter of disciplinary action from the board three years ago?" Pamela stopped and stared out the window while her mind traveled down memory lane, a lane she hoped to never be in again.

"Melanie isn't Trevor's wife. I think you know you're being extreme. She loves me, and that has very little to do with you." Brian stopped pacing in front of her desk, gripped the edge of the oversized mahogany credenza, and searched her eyes. "You're still punishing me, aren't you?"

"For what? Brian, you're a grown man. Please don't make this about you because it isn't."

"You know what I'm talking about. Me not wanting your advice about what happened with Penelope. Growing up, you were so focused on building your practice you didn't spend much time with me, and when you wanted to start being all nurturing and overly caring, I was fed up with the act. You couldn't handle the fact that I learned to deal with messy situations without my therapist mother. I guess while you were out fixing everyone else's problems, Dad helped me figure out my own mess."

"And what exactly are you saying?" Pamela's previously relaxed stance became more rigid and defensive. She leaned forward in her seat.

"You're punishing me for not being the adoring son when you were ready to be a mother."

She closed her eyes for a moment and inhaled deeply and slowly.

"Are you telling me you feel like I neglected you?" Pamela asked calmly.

Brian stepped away from her desk and took a seat on the dreaded patient couch. "Momma, sometimes it feels like I don't even know you. I mean, the woman you were when Melanie came over for Christmas is a lot different than the woman I've come to know. Where is she?"

"Brian, if there's something you'd like to say to me, please say it. Don't accuse me of anything or treat me like I know why you're angry. That's not going to help us heal." There was that calm therapeutic voice again.

"We don't have the kind of relationship I'd like to have. I feel like something is missing. Do you know how hard it was for me to find a gift for you? Sometimes I feel like I don't even know you, and I honestly don't know why that is. For a long time, I've been blaming you for it," Brian said thoughtfully. Something about sitting in front of his mother on her patients' couch made his vulnerability to emerge.

"Now, that I can work with. I can work with honest. Brian, I'm sorry if I've done anything that has made you feel like you're being punished or that you feel what I've done has driven a wedge between us. You're my only son, and all I've ever wanted was the best for you. All of your life, every choice I've made is proof of that." She rose and took the seat next to him on the couch. "I love you more than anything, and if you don't know that then I've failed somewhere." Her voice cracked and his heart shattered more.

"I love you, too, Mom."

"Since you're feeling like you don't know me, we can start our weekly lunches again when you're not busy."

"I'll do my best to make time for that."

"I can appreciate that. You're always so busy that your father and I hardly ever get a chance to see you. I was happy on Christmas Day because I finally had you in my sight for more than an hour without you running off because of a text or phone call." She put one arm around his shoulder and squeezed. He stiffened a bit then relaxed. He wasn't accustomed to her affection, yet her hug made his heart swell.

"There's still Melanie. I love her, Mom, and I'm happier than I've been in a long time. You have to know I won't stop seeing her."

"I knew you wouldn't. That's why I contacted the board to tell them about the situation myself. I couldn't have this biting me in the butt."

"Well, why did you tell her to leave me, then?"

"I didn't say 'leave' you. I said if she wanted to continue seeing me, then her choice would be to leave you. But still, she was heartbroken, and it hurt me to suggest it because I knew it would hurt you, and I know how she feels about you. You must understand I was only doing my job. My intentions were never to hurt either of you. You get that?" Pamela squeezed his hand tightly.

"I get it. What did the board say?"

"We're all good. I'd just rather be on the reporting side of things to keep myself clear of any entanglements." She left his side and walked a few steps over to her desk to retrieve her phone, pulled up the e-mail response from the board, and handed him the phone. He scanned the message and gave it back.

"Thanks, Mom. I'm glad we talked about this. I feel a lot better now."

Did he want his mom to get into any kind of trouble? No. But that thought wasn't going to stop him from being with Melanie. Whatever it took to help her, he'd do it. No one or nothing would stand in his way of being with her. Brian didn't show he cared enough when he dated Penelope, he didn't plan to make that same mistake with Melanie. He donned his coat and Atlanta Falcons beanie and gave his phone a quick check for messages.

"I asked Melanie to stop by, I hope you don't mind. It was necessary that you and I talked before settling things with her. It's important that she knows and understands what's going on, Mom."

"That's fine with me. When are you expecting her?" Pamela took a seat behind her desk.

"She's pulling up now. I'll go out to meet her and come right back."

Brian met Melanie at the elevator bank and pulled her into a tight squeeze the moment she stepped out of the double doors.

"I'm glad you were able to make it. I think there's something you need to hear. I don't want things to be awkward between you and my mom. You're important to me, so let's clear the air."

Brian kissed the top of her head and held on to one hand while they strode in unison down the dimmed corridor to his mom's office. Brian didn't knock or wait to be allowed back inside. He led Melanie straight through the privacy door and stopped at the wooden door, which proudly boasted a nameplate, Dr. Pamela Williams.

"We're back," Brian called and tapped on her door. He entered with Melanie at his side.

"Melanie, it's good to see you again." Dr. Williams greeted her with a warm genuine smile, more like the person Melanie spent the Christmas holiday with. "Please have a seat."

Melanie sat with perfect posture on the sofa next to Brian and crossed her ankles. Brian took her hand in his and she relaxed her shoulders only slightly, intent on listening to whatever his mom had to say.

"It's nice to see you. How are you?"

"Great. Let's talk a little more in depth about our last conversation," Dr. Williams began and explained the situation with Trevor, a former client of hers, without divulging his name. "I do know your situation is different, but I didn't want to take any chances. My career is important to me, and I know how important you are to Brian. Trust me, him bringing you over for Christmas dinner speaks volumes."

"Mom, let's not go there," Brian interrupted.

"All I'm saying is I believe you two are good for each other, and your relationship will only grow. Ending our doctor-patient relationship is the best thing I could do for you at this time. Does this make sense? My intent was not to hurt you in any way. I'm simply looking out for all of us."

"Understood. I must admit the separation hurt me, but I know it's for the best. I think continuing would be awkward anyway. I can't lie down on your couch and talk to you about Brian," Melanie half-joked and immediately wished she could rescind her comment. Though true, she was no longer under Dr. Williams' care but could sense the analyzation.

"Say no more. I wish you well, my dear." Pamela threw her palms in the air, stood, and pulled Melanie into an embrace. "You two have to get going. I have an appointment in about fifteen minutes."

"Thanks, Mom. I'll call you later."

"Come here." Pamela embraced Brian for at least a full minute. "I love you, son," she whispered.

Brian and Melanie left her office hand-in-hand at a much slower pace than when they arrived. Emotional weight lifted off their shoulders.

Free.

Free to move forward in their relationship.

Free to love without emotional hindrances.

Chapter 22

Freezing raindrops pitter-pattered on the ground rhythmically creating a tune that lulled Melanie into a relaxed state. She had her first session with her new therapist, Dr. Wang, and that went well. In fact, she had already taken Dr. Wang's advice to incorporate self-care into her routine more often, and today, that involved her curled up on her sofa with the latest romance novel from her favorite author, blanket draped across her knees, sipping a cup of coffee infused with her caramel creamer. Clean house. No work. Her favorite kind of Monday. She made a mental note to thank Pamela for the recommendation.

Her relationship with Brian was on an uptick, and she couldn't be happier. Once again, they talked daily, even if work kept them busy enough not to see each other.

The incessant ringing of her cell phone interrupted her reading. Brian. Though she loved him, they would have to have a talk about reading time. Her me time.

"Hey, you," she answered with a smile. Agitated or not, she welcomed an interruption from him.

"Hey. Enjoying your day off?"

"Yeah. How's your day going?"

"Even better now that I can hear your voice. Can I steal you away for lunch, or do you have other plans?"

"Lunch sounds good. What are you thinking?"

"Some really good southern food would be nice. Or Italian?"

"Anything sounds good right about now. I had a pretty early breakfast this morning."

"*Hmmm.* I have an idea. Are you in the mood for surprises?"

Melanie chuckled. Seeing him was good enough, but she said, "Sure. What time should I expect you?"

"I'll need a couple of hours. Can you hold out until about one-ish?"

"Yeah, that's fine." She smiled and bit her lip in anticipation.

"Good. See you in a bit, sweetie."

"Looking forward to it." Her smile broadened. He had a way of making her feel like a bowl of mush or a teenage girl with her first crush. She looked down at her attire and wondered if she should change. Right now, a pair of yoga pants and her alma mater's alumni t-shirt kept her comfortable. She decided against changing into something else and would wait until she heard from Brian about where they were going before she dug through her closet. For now, she'd open her book to the last page she'd read and pick up where she'd left off.

∞

Brian had taken the day off to relax. He'd gone into the office and spent a couple of hours there before deciding he needed another break to sort through his thoughts. After he made it home, all he could think about was Melanie. It had been about three days since he'd last saw her, much too long as far as he was concerned. Taking her out to lunch would be nice, but he did that often. The idea dawned on him —he'd never cooked for her. Now would be the perfect opportunity.

Grilled shrimp and fish had been favorites she'd mentioned in previous conversations. He would have to improvise and use his indoor grill, which he packed up in his truck on his way to the grocery store. He had planned to make the meal at home but cooking at Melanie's place would give them more time together. He dashed into the grocery store to gather ingredients to make shrimp kabobs, grilled salmon, rice pilaf, and sautéed lemon-butter spinach.

An hour later, he knocked at her door with one hand and a recyclable bag filled with groceries in the other.

"Hey. You're about an hour early," Melanie said when she opened the door.

"Disappointed?"

"No, no, come in. What's in the bag?"

"Lunch."

"I thought…" Her words trailed off.

"This is your surprise. I'm cooking for you. That's okay, right?"

"Absolutely. Be my guest." Melanie led him through the living room into the open-concept kitchen. "You can just set your stuff on the island. Can I help with anything?"

"Nope. This is my treat to you. Be right back though." Brian made a run to the car to grab his indoor grill.

"You can use this." Melanie held up a pink polka-dotted apron with the words *Kiss the Cook* stitched across the front.

He chuckled and put it on. "Just this once, and only for you."

"So cute." Melanie chuckled, secured the string with a bowtie, and snapped a picture of him with her phone. "Okay, the pans are here, the utensils are here, and the spices are here." She walked around tapping the designated white cabinets.

"Thanks."

"Are you sure there's nothing you'd like me to do?" Melanie leaned over the bag to see the contents.

"I'll take coffee if you have it."

"Aye, aye captain." She saluted him and filled the Keurig with water before popping in a coffee cup. She put his coffee mug on a coaster and took a seat at the counter-height pony wall and watched him maneuver around her kitchen.

"So, we're having shrimp and what else?"

"Salmon."

"*Oooh,* sounds delish. I can't wait. My stomach is rumbling at the thought of it."

"I only hope to live up to your expectations, ma'am." He turned to bow before her.

"You've far exceeded them up until this point. I don't see that changing now."

He walked over and lifted her hand to his lips and brushed the back of it with a gentle kiss. "I don't plan on it. With each passing day, I want you to think, *I can't get enough of Brian.*" He placed his hand over his heart, and she burst into laughter.

"It's too late for that."

His eyebrows shot up in response.

"Well, the only thing left for me to do is marry you to appease your wishes. That way, you'll have me every single day."

"That's a thought I can get with."

"Seriously? You don't think even the thought of marriage is too soon?" He took the seat next to her on the barstool and cupped her hands into his.

"In the world's eyes maybe, but I can't help how I feel."

"And I'm the man you can see yourself with forever. Wait, let me rephrase that: Am I the man you want to be with for the rest of your life?"

She kissed him and murmured against his lips, "Yes. Brian, I have never felt this way about anyone else, and I don't want to. I want to be with you."

Brian heaved a sigh of relief. "You're the only woman I ever want in my life, Mel. I haven't been able to get you out of my mind from the moment I first laid eyes on you. I want forever with you, but I don't want to rush you in any way. No pressure. I'm not going anywhere. I do love you."

"I love you, too, Brian. But you know what?"

"What's that?"

"My stomach is still growling," she whispered.

He chuckled and stood. "I get the picture. I'm on it. It's my pleasure to serve you."

"I'll stay here and keep you company though," she added and winked.

Brian washed his hands and then the fish before he added seasoning, which he called his secret weapon. He turned his back to her so she couldn't see what he used. He said he would only tell her after she had taken her first bite. Other than that, he moved around the kitchen freely and comfortably.

"Your mom taught you to cook, right?"

"Yeah. I watched her from time to time and my grandmother when she was alive. They were both adamant about not raising a helpless man. Granny said she wanted me to marry for love and not because I wanted or needed someone to wait on me hand and foot."

"Seriously?" Melanie giggled at the reference. Her grandmother would always fuss because she said her grandfather wanted her to wait on him hand and foot. Her own grandmother had cautioned her about not starting something she couldn't finish. "Melanie, don't start nothing for a man that you don't intend to do for the rest of his life. If you don't plan on making his plate every day, don't do it. If you don't plan on making him breakfast and coffee every morning, don't start it. If you don't plan on washing and folding his drawls, don't start it. Look here, if you start and stop, he'll be thinking something is wrong with you and not him. He'll just throw his laziness back on you, sayin' you spoiled him, which he might be right, but it doesn't give him no reason to not do anything for himself. That was your granny's mistake. I thought I was being a good wife by doing those things for ya pawpaw, and now look at him. He won't even fix his own plate. He'll near starve before he moves a finger and spoon some soup into this bowl. Be very careful about what you start," she'd told Melanie who was only ten years old at the time and had no idea why her grandmother would even be having that type of conversation with her at that age. Talking to Brian now had it all making sense.

"Very serious. As a kid, I snapped peas, picked, and washed greens, and learned what vegetables to pair with meats. Granny even taught me about seasonings and spices. I've also learned a lot by looking up recipes online, but my foundation came from Granny Mae and Momma."

"Well, if this is good, I'll have to send your momma a thank-you note."

"Or you can just kiss the cook." He pointed to the apron he wore.

"I'll take option B." She blew a kiss, which he caught and put in his pocket. "For someone who has claimed to have a limited skill set in the kitchen, you sure do sound like you know more than I do."

"I may be rusty since I tend to keep things simple. Grill or bake my choice of meat, add rice or potatoes, and a vegetable."

"I can make sure you get enough practice if that's what you need."

Brian smiled one of those I'll-give-you-whatever-you-want kind of smiles and Melanie reciprocated.

As he cooked, they talked about their desire for children, which they mostly agreed to except Brian wanted five and she desired two. Brian wanted his children to grow up with many siblings so they wouldn't have to be alone and would always have someone to count on, whereas Melanie thought two children were enough for multiple reasons. Nearing thirty-five years old meant she could have potential complications as she grew older. And if she were younger, she could get with the idea of four instead of two, but she had to consider her career and the stress pregnancy would put on her body. Besides, anything more than two, and they'd be outnumbered.

Brian's presentation was chef-like. If the food tasted anything like it looked, Melanie was about to be a happy camper. He'd plated everything perfectly, accompanied with glasses of sweet tea. He took off the apron, folded it, and placed it on the granite counter. He set the plates at the dining table and beckoned Melanie to have a seat.

Brian pulled out her chair and slid it to the table once she sat. "Your linner awaits, my lady."

"Linner?"

"Yes. Lunch and dinner. We're a bit overdue for lunch, so this is linner."

Melanie chuckled a bit. "I'll take it."

He took the seat next to her and joined hands with her to pray. "Father God, thank You for allowing us to share time and space with each other. Thank You for all Your blessings. Please bless our food to nourish and strengthen us. In Jesus' name. Amen."

"Amen."

Brian watched Melanie dip her fork into the salmon and bite. She smiled and moaned; her face lit with pleasure.

Yes.

Mission accomplished.

"Brian, this is amazing! It's so good." Melanie took another bite.

"Thank you. I'm glad you like it." He smiled, but this smile was different. It was a love-laced smile. If his heart swelled any more it would tear a hole in his chest. The pleasure plastered across her face was contagious and seeing he could elicit that type of response from her made him fall in love even more.

The look he wanted to give her forever.

"I think I'm officially spoiled now. I'm hiring you right this instant to be my personal chef. How much?"

"I only require one thing, which you can freely give." Brian gave her that look again. The look that made her mouth dry, her heart beg for more space, and her legs as unstable as a house built of gelatin. Good thing she was seated.

Melanie swallowed and with controlled breaths and measured words, asked, "And that is?"

"Your love. For your love, I'll do anything for you." He relinked his hand in hers, and she slid closer to press her lips into his.

No coming back from this day, this moment.

Chapter 23

Brian battled with the idea of partnering with Shane to start their own detective agency. Excitement brewed within him, yet marrying Melanie was at the forefront of his mind. Was it wise to get married and start a new business at the same time? Melanie needed stability and not the increased stress starting this business would cause.

He'd gone about his days solving cases as he'd done in the past, but now he saw his work from a distinct perspective. What would it be like to do this on his own and choose the type of cases he worked once the business became profitable? Investigating homicide cases would be history. Travel could be a possibility, though time away from Melanie wasn't appetizing, but the thrill of having control over what he pursued solidified his answer.

∞

"What's up, man?" Shane shifted his laptop bag into one hand and greeted Brian near the hostess station at Olive Garden with a one-arm handshake and hug.

"You tell me. You get a table yet?"

"I just walked in." Shane turned to the hostess. "Just two, please." They followed the hostess to a small booth near the back of the restaurant and ordered glasses of water before she walked away with the customary saying that their waitress would be by soon to take their orders.

Shane pulled his laptop out along with a folder he handed to Brian. "Ready to talk about this?"

"Yep. What do you have for me?"

"Take a look at this spreadsheet." Shane directed Brian's attention to his laptop, which showed what their start-up costs would be: rental space based on three different locations, advertising and marketing, ideas for a business name, and the advantages of forming an LLC versus a partnership.

"You've done quite a bit of legwork."

"Yeah, but there's more to be done. We'd have to work on our business plan to make sure it's solid."

Brian took a few moments to read through the folder with Shane's proposal, nodding in agreement along the way.

"What does Chloe have to say about this, with you being a newlywed and all? It's been about a year now, right?"

"Yeah. She's supportive. Her concerns are the same as any sane person would have—you know, what if it doesn't work, and what's my backup plan."

"And that is?"

"If it doesn't work, I'll return to the force," Shane stated matter-of-factly, "but I have a strong feeling we won't have to do that. This is what I envision: I'll spend the next year researching and gathering all the information I need and working on a business plan. In one year, I'll take an early retirement. I have enough saved up where I can afford to live off it for a couple of years while our business becomes established. And we really won't have many startup costs. Lease space and marketing will be the bulk of our expenses, but we could even hold off on leasing a space and work from home while we get started. And just think about it — we've already made a ton of connections throughout our careers at this point. I think we can make a go of it and do really well, man."

Shane was as excited as a man ready to welcome his first child into the world as he spoke about their potential to run a private detective agency. Brian nibbled on bread, something he hardly ever did, but the smell of the fresh breadsticks coupled with him internalizing Shane's proposal made it hard for him to resist.

"Everything you're saying sounds good, and from what you have in the proposal here seems solid." Brian tapped the manila folder.

"I'm sensing a 'but.' What's the problem?" Shane rested his back against the cushioned booth, preparing for rejection.

"I want to start a life with Melanie, and I don't know if this is how we should start. I could put in for early retirement, and I have some savings, but I don't want to worry her. I want her to feel secure in knowing I'm going to take care of her."

"Time out. Time out." Shane pointed his fingers into the palm of his other hand to form a *T*. "What? Is it *that* serious already?"

"Yeah, man."

"Look at you. You've got it bad, too, brother. I think I see hearts in your eyes. Have you talked to her about the career move?"

"Nah, not yet. I wanted to make my mind up about it first."

"And have you?"

"I think so. I like what I'm hearing and the possibilities. I'm in." Brian confirmed his agreement with a handshake.

"My man. One little piece of advice: No matter what the situation is, just talk to her. You never know how open and understanding she'll be about this or anything else if you don't, and congratulations."

"For what?"

"This. Melanie. And whatever else you two have going on."

"I'll take it. Thanks, bro."

They signaled the waitress who they'd waved off several times while they discussed business. Shane ordered chicken scampi, and Brian ordered lasagna. While they waited, they talked about their business plan a little more and the services they'd offer such as background checks, surveillance, missing persons, fraud investigations, bounty hunting, and stolen property. Their marketing tasks consisted of information gathering about their competitors. Even after their food arrived, their conversation centered around their new firm and whether they should consider a third business partner. They threw out names without deciding, determining they would pray about it before proceeding with that idea. Before dinner ended, they'd even decided on the name of their new private detective agency: PEyes, LLC.

Long after they said their good-byes and parted ways, Brian's invigoration lingered. He called Melanie and spoke to her for a while, but not about the business idea. That was a face-to-face conversation, and it was too late to show up at her door. He and Shane didn't leave the restaurant until after nine o'clock, so he headed home to get ready for work the next morning. Besides, he was on call, and he never knew when that rest would be interrupted.

After he showered and got in bed, sleep evaded him, though the pillowtop mattress and memory foam pillow usually did the trick. He sat up in bed, turned on the lamp, and grabbed his Bible from the nightstand and thumbed through the verse finder to read Scriptures relating to the plans of God. He then prayed God would lead him and Shane in the business plans and creation, and as usual, his prayers always ended up with God guiding him in his relationship with Melanie.

"Heavenly Father, thank You for the opportunity to come to You with anything that's on my heart. Forgive me for anything I've done, said, or thought that was contrary to Your Word, Lord God. Thank You for Your Word that reminds me You'll guide me along the best pathway for my life and that You'll work everything out according to Your purpose, so I entrust this private detective agency to You, God, and ask that You guide us in all of our decision-making. I know Your Word says, "A man who finds a wife finds a treasure, and he receives favor from the Lord," so I ask that You lead me in my relationship with Melanie, that I don't move too fast or too slow, but that everything happens in Your time. I want to do right by her and to be led by You. Watch over her, Lord, and be her shield of protection. Bless her home and her work, her going in and her coming out. Let no harm come near her and allow me to be who You would like me to be in her life. In Jesus' name. Amen."

After he prayed, Brian found himself able to rest. He committed to talk to Melanie about his and Shane's plans. Though sold this business decision could be a good move for him, he sought and desired her blessing. She had become increasingly important in his life, and her being okay with the idea would make all the difference in the world to him.

Chapter 24

Melanie sang and swayed to one of her favorite Brian McKnight love songs, which happened to make her think about *her* Brian. Tomorrow was Valentine's Day, and she had already mentally picked her black dress and matching pumps. She restocked her shampoo and conditioner and toweled down the sink bowl, her normal routine before she closed her shop for the evening. This was a late Wednesday for her. Wednesdays were normally short days, but Charise had an out-of-town date planned for Valentine's Day, and she'd asked to change her appointment.

Melanie dried her hands on the towel tucked in her smock and lifted the dryer to check Charise's style.

"A few more minutes."

Charise's normally chatty self was preoccupied with her phone under the dryer, though that didn't usually stop her from shouting across the room.

Melanie's head whipped ninety degrees and her heart leaped at the tap on the door. Brian was the only person who would show up to surprise her. She touched up a few loose strands in the mirror and answered the door.

"Oh, hi. Can I help you?" Melanie's smile waned and her chest deflated like someone had taken a needle and popped her balloon. Instead of the man she hoped to see, a young twenty-something with wild hair in desperate need of a trim stood at her door.

"Hi. I'm only in town for a few days, and a friend of mine recommended Lisa who works down the hall, but she can't take me. Can you please squeeze me in?" She shifted nervously from one foot to the other.

"I'm sorry, but I'm finishing up my last client for the evening. Why don't you try Tangie?" Melanie pointed to the closed door across from hers.

"I know it's late, and I'm not a client of yours, but I have a date tomorrow with my boyfriend. See?" She held up her phone to show Melanie his picture. "It's Valentine's Day, and I don't want him to see me looking like this." She fingered her poorly highlighted stringy, dry tresses. "Can you please help me? Please? I don't want anything special, just a wash and curl." She shook her head. "My hair isn't that thick, so it won't take long to dry. Please say you'll do it."

Melanie looked from her to Charise who she thought wasn't listening.

"Go on, Mel, I'll stick around and keep you company, if you want."

"Just a wash and curl?" Melanie surveyed her. Her hair was in desperate need of care and earning extra money never hurt.

"That's all." The young woman crossed her fingers and smiled with gritted teeth.

"Okay, come on in. What's your name?"

"Felissa. Like Melissa, but with an 'F.'"

"Well, it's nice to meet you, Felissa. I'm Melanie. Set your things on the loveseat and sit at the shampoo bowl," Melanie instructed, though still a bit reluctant to take her. She wanted to get home so she could wash and style her own hair for tomorrow, pick out her clothes, paint her nails, use her charcoal face mask, and take a bubble bath.

All things you can still do when you're done. You can do this quickly.

Felissa talked about her trip to Nashville from Louisiana and how she'd met her boyfriend Charles online last year. She gushed over him and about how in love she was and how she hoped he would be popping the question tomorrow. In between mentions of Charles and her love for celebrating Valentine's Day, Felissa repeatedly thanked Melanie for taking her as a walk-in.

Melanie nodded and encouraged the conversation with her occasional use of the word *really*. In five minutes, she'd completed Felissa's wash and conditioner. She motioned for Charise to sit in the stylist chair, and Felissa took Charise's vacated seat under the dryer.

"You're quiet this evening," Melanie said when she began styling Charise's hair.

"A lot on my mind, I guess."

Melanie stopped and spun the chair so Charise faced her. "Are you okay? Is there anything I can do for you?" Melanie touched Charise's forehead with the back of her hand.

Charise waved her off. "Not unless you want to be a surrogate for me."

"What?"

"Jeff is ready for more kids, and I'm not. He keeps bringing it up, and it's driving me crazy. He isn't home with them all day like I am, so I don't think he fully understands how much it takes to care for babies. I'm just not ready."

"That's sort of a good problem to have," Melanie teased. "You could be like me, wanting kids and still waiting to get married to have them." Melanie spun Charise around to continue styling her hair.

"Ah, girl, the way Brian is moving, you'll be married and close to having baby number one by this time next year. Ouch!"

"Sorry. My hand must've slipped."

"Ummm-hmmm."

Felissa's eyes shot up from her phone at Charise's squeal and interjected how much she wanted kids as soon as she married Charles. She told jokes about her nieces and nephews, to which Melanie and Charise chuckled. Melanie couldn't shake the feeling something seemed off about her. Considering she didn't know them well, Felissa discussed her relationship with Charles and his family — details Melanie wouldn't feel comfortable sharing with anyone she'd met within the hour. Melanie pushed back the awkward feeling that nagged in the pit of her belly and chalked it up to the fact that she was semi-annoyed because she intended to be on the road home by now.

"Alright, honey, I'm done," Melanie announced twenty minutes later and turned Charise toward the mirror to approve her style. Melanie fixed a loose strand here and there before Charise moved to an empty chair.

Melanie turned off Felissa's dryer and led her to the stylist chair. She blow dried Felissa's damp hair, clipped her raggedy splitting ends, and started her wrist magic with the curling iron. Every other curl, Felissa turned to check her hair in the mirror but continued to share stories about her nieces and nephews or her boyfriend. Felissa was right, it wouldn't take long to curl her hair. Fifteen minutes. Pleased with the outcome, Melanie turned Felissa to face the mirror.

"Wait. What are you doing?" Felissa dodged the finishing spray Melanie spritzed on her hair.

"What is it? You don't like the spray?"

Felissa picked up Melanie's comb from her styling tool tray like she was prepared to restyle her hair. "Nah. Can you fix this piece of hair here?"

Melanie took the curling iron and curled the strand tighter.

"And this one?" Felissa pointed to the top of her hair.

Melanie tightened up the curl and repeated the pattern another five times, something Melanie thought was unnecessary. Charise agreed according to her scowl.

"You don't like it?" Melanie started to experience a case of déjà vu. There had been only one other time in her career when she had a customer like Felissa.

"No, no, I don't, and I just can't see myself paying for something I don't like." Felissa picked at her curls with the feather comb.

"What do you mean?"

"I mean, I'm not paying for this."

"You owe me fifty dollars, Felissa." Melanie's pulse escalated, and she forced an even tone and smile.

"No, I'm not paying for anything I don't like. I'm getting out of here."

"You know what…you're right. You don't have to pay for anything you don't like." Melanie grabbed the nearest setting lotion bottle and soaked Felissa's hair to ruin her style.

Felissa jerked forward and screamed. "What are you doing?"

"Well you said you didn't like it. I'm not about to let you walk out of my shop with a style you don't like."

Felissa leapt out of the styling chair and stormed out of Melanie's shop screaming obscenities.

Charise's eyes were wide, and her mouth formed an O. "I can't believe you did that."

"Me either." Melanie flopped down in the styling chair, her hands shaking and her heart erratically thumping.

"But you did the right thing. She tried to stiff you."

Melanie slammed the spray bottle down on the shelf. "I knew it. I knew something was wrong with her when she walked in here. I just felt something off about her. She wasn't planning to pay for a style."

Charise walked over to hug her. "I'm sorry, especially since I encouraged you to take her."

"Thanks, honey. The good news is we're even now. We weren't going to have another case of Monique."

"Oh gosh, I remember that."

"Yes. I think that's what happened. That whole scene instantly took me back to when I first started working and looking to build my clientele. Monique waltzed into the shop, same as Felissa, needing a stylist. Everyone else was busy, so I took her. When I finished, Monique screamed that I messed up her hair and that she was never coming back."

Unlike Felissa, Monique walked out of the salon with the style. It wasn't until she meditated on the situation that Melanie realized she'd been duped.

Never again.

Felissa caught the wrong person.

"Honey, you've always been at the top of your game. I'm glad you didn't let that situation stop you, because I love what you do to my hair." Charise tossed her hair from side-to-side, showing off her glossy, weightless curls.

"Thanks for sticking with me all these years. You know I appreciate you." Melanie peeled herself from the styling chair. "Let me clean up."

"I'll help." Charise grabbed the broom and swept the last pieces of hair off the floor and wiped down the chairs. Melanie cleaned the sink again and put on her coat.

"Thanks, Charise. Go on home to Jeff and the kids. I've kept you long enough. He's probably worried since you don't usually stay as long."

"Yeah, but he's been texting me, so he knows I'm still with you. It's all good."

A gnawing sensation stirred in the pit of Melanie's belly, one she couldn't explain so she didn't mention it, though Charise's company brought her some level of comfort. Melanie locked up after they finished cleaning and walked alongside Charise to the exit at the end of the corridor.

Melanie embraced Charise, wished her a Happy Valentine's Day, and stepped into the cool evening air.

The motor of an older model Mustang revved up and raced toward her the moment she stepped into the parking lot. Every organ inside of her cringed and caused momentary paralysis. Charise sprinted to her side, grabbed her arm, and pulled her back onto the sidewalk. The Mustang swerved in their direction and jerked to a stop in front of them. Felissa, who occupied the passenger seat, lowered the window, and shouted, "Might wanna watch where you're going next time, nappy-headed wench!" Felissa flipped her middle finger, shouted a few choice obscenities, and cued the driver with a nod.

Melanie clutched her chest with one hand and Charise's arm with the other when the tires screeched and burnt rubber filled the air.

"That shook me a bit, Mel. Are you okay? Do you want to call Brian? He's a cop. I know there's something he can do."

Melanie turned slowly to look at Charise. Her lips parted, but no words came.

"Mel, you're shaking. Let's go back inside and call Brian."

"I'm okay. I just need a moment." Melanie shut her eyes and did three cycles of breathing exercises to calm her nerves. "I'll be okay. I think what bothered me the most is that fool had a gun."

"Felissa?"

"No, the driver. I don't think he was going to use it, but I'm sure I saw him wave it around. I guess he tried to scare me."

"Mel, I really think we ought to call Brian."

"I don't think there's anything we can do. Did you get the plate number? For all we know, her name may not even be Felissa. I'm sure she won't be back, and I won't take another walk-in again. Clearly those don't work in my favor."

"Maybe, but I'd feel better if you told Brian." Charise looked up and pointed to the building. "Don't you all have cameras around the building?"

Melanie shrugged. "I'm not sure, and the temperature is dropping. I'm ready to go home. Let's go."

"For all we know, that crazy thang might be waiting to follow you home. Let's call Brian to be on the safe side."

Melanie checked her watch. Six-forty-five. Later than she wanted to leave, but still time to relax and prepare for tomorrow. She took Charise's advice, called Brian, and tried to explain the situation to him. The moment she said she needed him, he was en route.

Charise waited with her until he arrived. Visibly relieved, she left Melanie in Brian's care after he escorted her to the parking lot.

"Tell me what happened," Brian insisted. He wrapped an arm around her shoulders and walked her to her car.

"Can we talk about it tomorrow? I'm exhausted and I want to go home and relax. I promise to give you all the details tomorrow."

"No."

"What? Why not?"

Brian stopped next to her car and took her hands in his. "It was serious enough for you to call me out here, so I need to know what's going on. Who do I need to handle for you?"

"Babe, we're good." Melanie wrapped her hands behind his head and her promising pupils gazed into his. "Trail me home. After I shower and eat, I'll call to talk with you about it. Is that better?"

"I'll take it." Brian gave her a quick peck on the lips. "Let's get you home."

Melanie made a mental note to thank Charise for insisting she call Brian. His voice alone wrapped her in comfort, but his presence promised protection and security. Nothing would ever happen to her as long as he was a part of her life.

Chapter 25

Brian chuckled heartily at the scene Melanie painted as she retold the story of Felissa in her salon earlier that evening. Now she could laugh about it, but earlier she was shocked and angry. The nerve of that woman trying to get over on her. She'd been duped before and that drove her to question her skill. The one good thing that came from Monique doing the same thing to her years before was she'd taken additional cosmetology classes to hone her craft. No one would ever have her question herself again. If they didn't like their style, it wasn't going to be because of something she did.

"I'm sorry that happened to you, sweetheart, but I can't get the image of you messing up anybody's hair out of my mind. I never took you to be feisty." Brian said through the constant chuckling. "And I'm not laughing at you, I'm laughing with you."

"*Ummm-hmmm.* Enough about my day. How was yours?" Melanie asked. She stood in front of her closet mirror and held her favorite black dress in front of her, turned from side to side, and struck several poses. Her wireless earphones made it easy for her to be hands free while she perused her closet. She thought she'd had her mind made up about what she would wear the next day, but when she went through her closet, she second-guessed herself.

"Nothing quite as exciting as yours. Mostly desk work today, which I'm grateful for since I needed to catch up on some file work. But that sounds like half of the story. Tell me what happened that sparked your call to me."

The scene she didn't want to relive. On the drive home and through most of her shower, she couldn't help but wonder *what-if.* What if the guy in the driver's seat fired the gun at her? And for what, not allowing his girlfriend to get a free hairstyle? She recounted the incident to Brian.

"Do you want to file charges? There are ways we can find this person. She could possibly be involved in other criminal activity."

"I'd like to forget this thing ever happened." Avoidance. Months of therapy taught her to deal with issues head-on, but this was one situation she'd like to erase from memory. "We're going out tomorrow night, so I'd much rather focus on our date. Is that okay?"

"Only if you're sure. If you feel differently tomorrow, let me know so we can take care of it. I don't want anything to happen to you, Mel."

"I know. She won't show up again. A person like her will probably go on to find someone else to take advantage of."

"And that's why I think you should press charges. The next person she has a run-in with could get hurt."

"If I change my mind, I'll file charges. I don't want to talk about that anymore. Where are we going tomorrow?" By this time, Melanie considered a red dress, thinking it might go along with the theme of Valentine's Day and love.

"I made reservations at a French restaurant about a month ago. Is that okay with you, or do you want something different? With every nice restaurant in town booked by now, I guess I should have asked sooner."

"That sounds good, but having you cook for me again would be even better." Her tone casual, and her attention fixated on what to wear. By now, she held the fifth dress since they'd been on the phone.

"You'd be okay with that on Valentine's Day?" Brian sounded surprised.

"Absolutely. You underestimate your skills, honey. That was one of the best meals I've had in a long time. I could go for more of what you have to offer."

"One of? So, what was the best meal you've ever had?"

"Hmmm." Melanie paused her dress search and sat on the brown tufted ottoman to contemplate his question. What was the best meal she'd ever had? As much as she loved food, it seemed that would have been an easy question to answer. "I was in Vegas for my friend's bachelorette party, and we ate at one of the hotel restaurants along the strip. I don't remember the restaurant, but I remember the meal: steak, potatoes, and asparagus,

which is a little odd because steak is probably the last thing I'd order off any menu, but the waiter talked me into it. It was grilled to perfection, somewhere in between medium well and well done. Tender. Juicy. And a little buttery. And the potatoes melted in my mouth. The asparagus blew my mind—first time I'd ever eaten asparagus when I had it that night. Oh, Brian, it was so good. I think I can taste it now."

"I think I want steak after hearing you talk about it like that."

"Yeah, it was good. And like I said, I'm not a steak person, and I don't think I've had it since then. It was delicious though."

"What would you like me to cook for you tomorrow?"

"Whatever you'd like. Tomorrow night is about us being together, but that isn't a pass to burn the food either. I still want something good, just not sure what, so surprise me."

"I can do that. Anything else I can do for you?"

What did he want her to say? Did he want an honest answer?

Honest would say kiss her like his life depended on it.

Honest would tell him to update his list of basic needs to include loving her.

"I'll let you know when I think of it."

"Let me get to planning, and I'll call you in the morning, Mel. I love you. Have a good night, and dream about me."

"You don't even have to tell me to dream about you, happens anyway. I love you, too. Good night." Melanie removed the wireless headset from her ears and resumed her task of looking for the perfect dress. This time, she hummed and danced in the mirror from excitement. She had a good feeling about tomorrow night, unsure of where it came from or to what it alluded. It could be she missed him and couldn't wait to see him again.

Their last date had been a few days ago, too long ago in her book.

∞

Brian scanned recipes on his tablet. He'd done fish already and leaned toward steak, but Melanie said that wasn't her favorite meal. He could imagine the look of pure pleasure on her face as she talked about the best steak she'd ever had, the same look she had when she ate the meal he'd prepared for her. Eyes closed and a smile spread across her face with her bottom lip tucked between her teeth. An image that had been hard to forget. He'd for sure prepare the steak for her another time.

He selfishly wanted his steak to be the one she thought of when thinking of her favorite.

It wasn't extremely cold, but he figured he could pull off a romantic dinner in front of the fireplace, and with that idea, serving pasta came to mind. He searched the phrase *romantic dinner ideas* and became overwhelmed with all the information in his feed.

Lemon garlic pasta with shrimp, garlic bread, and parmesan-crusted green beans caught his attention. Brian checked the time. Ten o'clock. As far as dessert, he wouldn't have time to prepare it and dinner, so unless his mom had an idea for a quick dessert it would come from the bakery section at his local grocery store.

He video called her.

"Hey, Mom. What are you up to?"

"Getting ready for bed. Are you okay? You never call after nine o'clock."

"Change of plans for tomorrow evening. I'm cooking for Melanie and was hoping you could give me some dessert ideas. Something that wouldn't take too much time." Brian rattled off the dinner menu.

"Depends on how romantic you're trying to be."

Brian pulled the tiny velvet box out of his pocket, opened it, and showcased the ring.

Pamela screamed, shuffled her feet in place, and turned the phone screen toward Stanley who smiled proudly and nodded his appreciation after he got a glimpse of the ring. "So, you're going all the way out? Congratulations, son. I love Melanie for you. I'm so excited I can't think straight anymore."

"Thanks. That means a lot to hear you say that."

Pamela dabbed at her eyes with the knuckle of her index finger. "Chocolate-dipped strawberries will work if you want to keep it simple. Feels a little less guilty, too, because of the fruit factor."

Images of him feeding strawberries to Melanie in front of the fireplace filled his mind.

Strawberries it is.

"That's exactly what I'm looking for. I'll let you guys get some rest. Thanks. Talk to you later."

"We love you."

"Love you all, too. Good night."

He ended the call and examined the diamond ring in the small velvet box.

Tomorrow would change his life forever.

Chapter 26

Valentine's Day had been a holiday Melanie could have done without in the past. *Indifferent* is how she would describe her feelings toward it. To her, it was like any other day, and she didn't see the reason why people went through such great lengths to spend tons of money to prove their love for their significant other on one day of the year.

For her, love was a daily attitude and action, not something that could be expressed with a bouquet of overpriced roses and an expensive dinner. And while she still felt the same way today about it, excitement ripped through her, and she couldn't quite explain why.

Usually, she'd listen to random songs and stations on the radio while she worked and often changed the station to suit her clients' tastes. But today, she had her own playlist in rotation. She'd connected her Bluetooth so she could hear some of her favorite artists serenade her with love songs, all songs that made her think of Brian, heightening her anticipation for the evening. At least three of her clients commented on the music choice, asking if she was in love, to which she gave the same response every time: "Now more than ever."

She'd purposefully planned a short day. Some of her usual clients arranged for earlier appointments which helped her plan fall into place perfectly. She'd finally decided on the right dress for the evening, and all she had left to do was curl her hair after her final appointment. She received several messages from Brian throughout the day, teasing her of what was to come later that evening. The infusion of emotions overwhelmed her.

Melanie prided herself on the fact that she wasn't moved by roses and fancy gifts, but when she pulled into her driveway, she spotted a large bouquet of roses sitting on the white bench near her front door, awaiting her arrival. She quickly climbed out of the car and walked on shaky legs to the bench. The chill in the air would have normally ushered her into the house, but her astonishment froze her tracks. Her hands trembled and her heart's steady beat had lost its rhythm when she removed the note from the bouquet and read, *The beauty of these roses represent everything that's taking place in my heart. Our love is beautiful, and my hope is that it'll bloom forever. I love you, Brian.*

Every part of her now trembled. She fumbled with the key to open the door. She took the roses to the kitchen and set them on the granite counter near the window. Why was she so nervous? They were just flowers, and she didn't care much about flowers, but the man who sent them. She pulled her cell phone from her purse to call Brian.

"Did you get my message?"

Her stomach quivered when his deep voice came on the line. His voice in and of itself was love. A love her ears, heart, mind, and spirt had committed to memory and never wanted to do without.

"If you're talking about the flowers, then yes. Thank you. How did you know no one would come by the porch and swoop them up?"

"I didn't, but I was willing to take a chance. I tried to time it to where they wouldn't be out there for too long. Do you like them?"

"They're beautiful. Thank you for thinking of me."

"I'm always thinking of you. I have more in store for you tonight. Think of that as your appetizer."

Melanie smiled from ear to ear. "All right, Mr. Morris, don't start anything you don't plan to keep up."

"I'd never do that. You'll learn soon enough that I intend to keep up everything I start."

The promises of his words and the intensity of his baritone voice left her speechless and her heart craving what was to come. Melanie was thankful her expression was concealed by the phone and he didn't have lenses to see the crazy gyration of her heart. Had she ever been in a position where her mouth hung open and no words came out?

"But I'll give you time to get ready. See you at seven?"

"Seven it is," Melanie managed to confirm.

A vision of Brian doting on her for years to come flashed through her mind. Something about the way he said, "you'll learn soon enough" sent a surge of currents through her core. That coupled with flowers she would have been fine without were the appetizer—and her heart could hardly handle it.

How would she manage the entrée?

∞

Brian went into the office for a couple of hours and took the rest of the day off to prepare the perfect evening for Melanie, an evening she would never forget. When he left the precinct, he headed straight to the grocery store to pick up the ingredients for that night's dinner. He hadn't planned to buy roses, but the grocery store advertised heavily. When he saw them, he immediately thought of Melanie and believed it would make an excellent addition to his evening plans. He carefully chose the bouquet and delivered it before she arrived home, risking damage by the weather or someone stealing them, but she wasn't expecting it, and at the very least, he wanted to be the reason for the smile on her face.

Mission accomplished.

He could feel her smile through the telephone receiver.

He cleaned his house and washed blankets before he arranged them on the floor for their dinner, another risk he took. He should have told her they'd be sitting on the floor, though he told her to dress comfortably. Either way, they could move to the floor for dessert if dinner by the fireplace didn't work. He showered, dressed, and began dinner preparations. Melanie rang his doorbell at exactly seven o'clock.

Perfect timing. Their pasta was boiling, and the bread was baking. Everything would be fresh and flavorful, just as he'd planned.

Brian advanced to the door at the sound of the doorbell dressed in black slacks and a red buttoned-down dress shirt. His breath caught in his chest at the sight of Melanie, dressed in a scoop-necked black dress with ruched sides and matching black pumps. Her natural ringlets were glossy and curled tight. Her light makeup included shiny lips, which his eyes rested upon.

"Beautiful as always. Come on in," he finally said after he stared at her for several seconds.

"Thank you. You look handsome tonight." Melanie inhaled. "*Ummm*. It smells good in here." She handed him her coat, set her purse on the couch, and walked into the kitchen. Atlanta Falcons décor was the theme in the living room and kitchen.

"Thanks. Gotta look my best for my lady." He winked. "Have a seat at the table while I finish up. Need something to drink?"

"Water is good for now." She took a seat at the round table with place settings and chairs for two, hugging her elbows. Stiff, like she'd never been inside his home.

Why was she acting like they hadn't been on umpteen dates?

"So, what's after dinner?"

"I can't tell you. I thought you said you liked surprises." Brian handed her a bottle of water and returned to the kitchen to finish dinner and prepare their plates.

"I do, but it's killing me."

"Can I distract you for a minute then? I want to talk with you about something."

Melanie shifted in her seat and adjusted her posture. "Sounds serious. Sure."

Brian shared the private detective agency idea with Melanie, gauging her reaction to every detail. She listened intently and encouraged him throughout with reassuring smiles and nods.

"I hadn't thought about it much until Shane mentioned it, but the more I think about it, I think this will be a great move for me."

Melanie propped her elbow on the table and rested her chin in her palm. "Have you prayed about it, Brian?"

"I have."

"And how do you think God is leading you?"

"I feel comfortable with the idea, and as of now, there hasn't been anything to suggest I shouldn't move forward with it."

"Then do it. Take a step of faith."

Brian prepared their plates with chef-like presentation again. He told her of his plans to have dinner in front of the fireplace.

"Seems so romantic. Of course." She squeezed her shoulders and sucked her bottom lip between her teeth.

"What about your dress? Will you be comfortable on the floor with it on? I can get more blankets if you'd like."

"Well, let me see first."

Brian led her to the covered area on the floor and flipped the switch to turn on the fireplace. She kneeled and made herself comfortable, wiggling around a bit. He handed her a pillow and cloth napkin.

"Is it comfortable for you, or do we need to sit at the table?"

"This will work."

"Okay. Be right back." He went to the kitchen to get her plate and a glass of sparkling white cider. When she was settled, he returned for his own dinner and drink. "Okay, let's pray. Heavenly Father, thank You for Your goodness and mercy on this day. We pray that our thoughts and hearts honor You. We ask that You bless our meal and our time together and that You be in the midst of us this evening. In Jesus' name. Amen."

"Amen."

He waited for her to take a forkful of food into her mouth before continuing their conversation. His heart warmed and his chest swelled at the look of pleasure on her face. No one was more suited for him than her.

"Good?" Brian smirked, raised one eyebrow, and anticipated her response.

"So good. *Ummm.* You are spoiling me."

"Solely my intent." He took a bite of his own food and gave himself a mental pat on the back.

"If I can be honest with you, the thing that bothers me most about starting a business right now is you."

"Wait, me?" Melanie squealed, her head cocked to the side with one eyebrow lifted. "What did I do?" Her fork was raised midway to her mouth, and her eyes enlarged.

"I should rephrase that." He cleared his throat. "I'm not sure if it's the right time to start a business and a marriage. I don't want you to worry about our future or stress about the business. I want you to be and feel secure, and I'll do everything in my power to make sure of it. It just seems like a tough promise to make if I don't know when I'll have my next client."

"That's a valid concern," she said slowly and thoughtfully, "but Brian, we aren't married yet, and we don't know if or when that'll happen, so try not to worry about that, and take a step of faith. Don't let me stop you. You did say you had a plan, and you have savings, right?"

"I did and I do, but clearly you don't see where I'm going with this." He chuckled nervously watching the light from the fireplace dance in her eyes. He set his plate to the side, reached into his pocket for the small velvet box, and positioned himself to kneel on one knee. "You're right. My concerns are valid because how you feel matters. You need to know I'll always do what I can to take care of you." He opened the box. "Melanie, being with you is the best thing that's happened to me, next to my salvation. Every decision I make, I want you to be a part of. I want you by my side forever. I love you, and I want to love you forever. Will you marry me?"

Melanie nearly choked on a parmesan-crusted green bean. She'd had a feeling he would propose, but she'd talked herself out of it, thinking it silly for the thought to even cross her mind, yet here she was. Her eyes filled with tears, and her breath caught in her throat.

"Yes. Yes, I will."

Brian slipped the ring on Melanie's finger, pulled her into a passionate embrace, pressed his lips against hers, gently yet fervently expressing his love for her with every move of his lips.

"Thank you. I'll do my best to always show you how much I love you."

Breathless, Melanie whispered, "I can't believe it. Brian! Was this my surprise?"

"Well, I'd planned to do it much later in the evening, but you left me no choice. I love you, and I always will, Mel."

"I love you, too, Brian." Melanie wrapped her arms around his neck and squeezed tightly.

Tonight was a dream come true, a Valentine's Day they would remember for the rest of their days.

I hope you enjoyed Melanie and Brian's journey! Melanie and Brian first met in Out of the Shadows (Love, Lies & Consequences book 4). Check it out if you haven't already! Please take a moment to leave a review.

I'd love to hear from you. Please connect with me on my website www.natashafrazier.com

If this is the first title you've read of mine, I encourage you to check out my catalogue.

Devotionals

The Life Your Spirit Craves

Not Without You

Not Without You Prayer Journal

The Life Your Spirit Craves for Mommies

Pursuit

Fiction

Love, Lies & Consequences

Through Thick & Thin: Love, Lies & Consequences Book 2

Shattered Vows: Love, Lies & Consequences Book 3

Out of the Shadows: Love, Lies & Consequences Book 4

Kairos: The Perfect Time for Love

Non-Fiction

How Long Are You Going to Wait?

About the Author

Natasha writes Christian fiction and devotionals. When she isn't reading or writing, she spends her time swimming or watching movies with her family. Natasha lives in the Houston metro area with her husband and three children. Connect with Natasha online:

Instagram @author_natashafrazier

Twitter @author_natashaf

Facebook @craves.2012

Website: www.natashafrazier.com